You, Me, and

Nobody Else

Joanne Schehl

ISBN 978-1-63630-955-2 (Paperback)
ISBN 978-1-63630-956-9 (Digital)

Covenant Books, Inc.
11661 Hwy 707
Murrells Inlet, SC 29576
www.covenantbooks.com

T hank you to my ever so patient Grandson David and his wife Rachel for helping me navigate the technology needed to bring my book to life.

Contents

Introduction

A step back in time, the fictitious Christian characters and plots taken from real-life events became a delightful challenge to merge them together into one entertaining novel. A dash of true local and national history adds to the flavor of this read.

The story is an insight into the American families' presence in the Northwoods of Wisconsin from the late 1920s through 2000. Their joy, hopes, adventures, and fears are portrayed in every paragraph. Each chapter is an individual tale along with an overall account of the lifetime of two characters who lived their lives with love and purpose.

It is my true desire for you to enjoy this adventure as much as I did when I wrote it. May your life be enriched by experiencing what this novel portrays.

Sincerely,
Joanne Schehl

CHAPTER 1

With a Gee! and a Haw!

Newly married on Columbus Day within the rules of tradition, my sweetheart carried me over the threshold. We fell on the floor.

"I tripped over your long dress. Should we try again?" Tony jested.

"No, silly, I'm not going to put my life in *your* hands. Dare you to chase me to the bedroom." Running off, I tripped over my own gown and tumbled head over heels. I laughed so hard my cheeks hurt.

Tony had built our home prior to engagement with wood harvested from his land. Once a cabin now stood a castle. While engaged, we remodeled and decorated to both of our tastes. Traditional for me and wildlife-inspired for him.

"I want to put a cross-stitched pillow in each corner of the couch and hang your mounted Musky on the wall," I said.

"Nice! You're the lady of this house. Make it look right. I don't have any idea where things should go, but I can hang a curtain rod or do a repair. You decide on the decorating."

My husband first moved to Wisconsin as an art student from Chicago. He planned to study and paint the beauty of the Northwoods. His fascination with the area kept him here. His father, a carpenter, taught him well. Using those skills, he supported himself and bought a four-acre parcel of land along the shoreline of EarShot Lake. He had built a sturdy home to last his lifetime.

Our family came to Wisconsin from Iowa. Father, a lumber camp cook, found time to build our bungalow in the town of Eagle River. I grew up in a community of two thousand people. You might call me a city girl. My parents still live there.

Every winter, I attended our town's Winter Carnival, where Tony and I met. My eyes kept track of him from the first glimpse. Imprinted in my mind as the most handsome man I had ever seen, I sought him out.

While at a rifle competition, he stopped me cold in my tracks. Did I recognize him? I knew everybody around here. How is it that I never met this man?

I asked my girlfriend, Sue, "Who is the blond in box 3?"

"Oh! Tony? He moved here from Chicago. Haven't you met?"

"No. He sure shoots well."

"A group of us plan to eat supper at the community center. He'll be there. Why don't you join us?"

"Count me in."

Sue introduced us. "Beatrice Hamilton, let me present Anthony Weston."

"Glad to meet you, Beatrice Hamilton," he said with a twinkle in his eyes.

Up close, he looked even more handsome. Blond strands of hair covered half of his large baby blue eyes and complemented his soft-spoken voice and mannerism. His strong attraction to me became apparent when he invited me to sit alongside him. His gaze never flickered away from his contented smile. Like the intense concentration of a good jeweler, we couldn't take our eyes off each other until we parted after dinner. Fascination intensified as we dated.

Tony called me "Babe." He said the name fit my short stature, brown hair, and eyes. I called him Tony. It sounded natural. Grandmother always said, "Opposites attract."

Eighteen months later, he proposed while we stood under a large beach umbrella.

"Babe, what would you say if I asked you to marry me? We're good as a couple. I want to be with you all the time."

"What do you mean? Yes, of course. Have I been asked?" I teased.

I knew exactly what he meant. We made the proposal final when we picked out rings and set the date of Columbus Day, October 12, 1927, for our wedding.

When our first Christmas as a married couple drew near, we made an attempt to decorate for the holiday. You would expect I'd be happy, but I didn't feel joyful.

Why? I'm a new bride, my husband loves me, and we have a beautiful place to live. I tried to stop the tears when I went outside to feed the sled dogs. The clear moonlight sparkled off the fresh snowfall. The beauty of the night squelched my sadness. I missed my family. How could this be when I'm with my loving husband? Confused, I returned to the house, and once inside, my sad eyes hid in the flicker of the fireplace flames.

Whenever Tony wanted to discuss something with me, he always invited me to come sit close to him on the couch. He would pat the cushion alongside him and say, "Come sit with me. I want to talk to you." He always beckoned me for discussion this way. He did so when he called me from standing alongside the hearth. I obliged.

"Let's hook up the teams, go into town, and visit your parents. Maybe they'll spend the holiday week here. You miss them. We can bring both sleds. There will be enough seats for the four of us. We can bring them back here."

My wonderful husband understood how much I missed them! Sadness turned to joy. I bubbled with happiness. How did he know?

We bundled into our one-piece snowsuits, put the dogs' boots on, hitched the teams, and drove to town. The dogs' boots were made of animal skin. They kept slush and ice from building up between their toes.

While we traveled, Tony's voice carried through the woods as he shouted to the dogs, "Gee" to the right and "Haw" to the left. Fine snow blew in our faces as the rudders raced through drifts. Moonlight led the way.

My parents greeted us with open arms. Mom scrambled to make hot cocoa to serve with her holiday cookies, and Dad helped secure the dogs. The heat from the hearth warmed us while we visited.

"Babe and I would like to bring you to our place for the week. It would be nice for us to be together for the holidays. Would you like to come?" Tony asked.

"This could be fun. I'd love to come. I'll bring some of my jelly and cookies. Will this be okay?" Mother asked.

"Small game is open. We could hunt. I'll bring my gun," Dad answered.

We stayed overnight and packed in the morning. When done, we had little space left. Father drove the biggest sled, and we traveled in the smaller one. Again, Tony cracked the whip and yelled "Gee!" and "Haw!" The dogs' instincts carried us home.

We started the parade of winter holidays by attending services at our little church in Granite on Christmas Eve. There is no way to replace the sense of unity generated when the family is together. Mostly everyone in our community came. Parents displayed patience with their children who skipped from place to place in excitement of Santa's promised visit. Jesus's birthday brought love and peace to our little town.

We spent the holiday week enjoying our visit. Mom and I did some sewing and cooked some of our favorite dishes. Dad and Tony hunted almost every day. We were glad to store the extra meat in our icehouse.

New Year's Eve ushered in a nasty blizzard. Father voiced concern about the piles of snow on their roof and wanted to leave as soon as possible.

"With additional snow weight on my roof from this storm, I am concerned it might cave in. We shoveled yours last week when we first got here. You don't need to worry about yours," Dad said.

"We're not worried about our place, but you're right, we need to shovel yours as soon as we can. When it's safe to travel, we'll leave," Tony answered.

The winds calmed, and the storm ceased; we reevaluated.

"Snowdrifts are everywhere. Travel will be difficult because the roads are hard to see. Do you want to chance leaving now?" I asked.

"We'll take the chance. I need to get back as quick as I can," Dad said.

We loaded our gear, hooked up the teams, and headed out. Sporadic clouds followed us. The stillness echoed Tony's crack of the whip, with a "Gee!" and a "Haw!" Confused, the dogs sensed their lack of direction, and snow mounds blocked their regular path. They guided each other but barely stayed on track.

The snow on my parents' rooftop hung down in swirled loops.

"We're here on time. I'm ready to help," Tony said.

Dad had extra shovels. I took charge of one and joined them. We shoveled and shoveled and shoveled some more. Dad thanked us.

"I couldn't have done it in one day myself. If we didn't remove the weight right away, the roof might have collapsed."

"Glad to do it. The roof appears intact," I answered.

Mom cooked us a scrumptious dinner. Famished, we gobbled it down. Although tired, Tony and I decided to return home. We fed and hitched the teams and said our goodbyes.

The crack of the whip and "Gee!" and "Haw!" echoed across the snow-covered fields. It became music to my soul. When I hear this song, even today, it reminds me of the love and understanding Tony gave me, our first Christmas together.

CHAPTER 2

The Perfect Match

Tony noticed a disturbance on the lake through the window over our breakfast table while he ate his cinnamon roll.

"Look over by the spruce tree. It looks like a deer fell through the ice. I'm going outside and see if I can help the poor thing."

Putting on his boots and jacket, he said, "I'll be right back."

This day had started out like an ordinary day. Little did we know, Tony would meet one of the best friends of his lifetime.

I had decided to follow him and put on my coat and snowshoes and tracked him to the water's edge. I watched my hero walk cautiously over slippery ice to what appeared to be a fallen doe. Stuck and half submerged, she couldn't pull out of her death trap; the front part of her body stretched across the frozen glacier while her rear was squeezed through the cracked ice into the bitterly cold water.

"This deer is not going to freeze or starve to death on my watch," Tony said.

"Don't get any closer. I can see a difference in the color of the ice. You'll fall through," I warned.

Scared out of my wits for both of us, I took a timid step to try and get closer.

"Babe, get back before you fall in. Go to the garage, get all the rope you can find, and bring it to me."

"Okay."

Our county sheriff saw the struggle from the nearby shoreline. Pulling a sled covered with a variety of gadgets, he slid his way across the crystal-like surface to join us. Already on my way back, I returned with two long clotheslines and several lengths of rope.

"Stop where you are and just throw them over as far as you can," Tony yelled.

With a thrust and extended arms, the pieces sailed across the frozen glaze like a smooth ball in a bowling lane.

"Go back to the house. I've got enough help."

I took baby steps and returned. The house felt cozy and warm. I didn't need to be out there. I sat at the kitchen table and wrapped my hands around a hot coffee mug and watched the rescue.

Tony laid flat on his stomach across the slippery terrain. The sheriff used all his strength and know-how to help Tony get ropes around the front of the doe. They did not have enough traction to move the frantic animal in any direction. The sheriff walked to his sled for rug pieces to put underfoot for grip—the position held while they continued with their two-man rescue.

Neighbors saw the effort and wanted to help. They arrived with additional lines and equipment. With a bigger team of helpers, the rescue took place safely. The doe ran off, paused, tilted her head, and looked back as if to say thank you.

Once out of sight, the six-man team headed toward our back entrance. Snowy boots stacked alongside our door with hats, coats, scarves, and gloves announced our visitors. The neighbors warmed themselves by the fireplace. While sipping hot drinks, they talked about their adventure.

One by one, they rebundled and left. The sheriff, who we now knew as Jim, remained and said, "I like the way you handled things today and would like to talk with you about a job opportunity."

Surprised, Tony's eyes popped with heightened eyebrows.

"A job? What kind?"

The three of us sat around the kitchen table.

"You and I think a lot alike, and I need someone I can work with as my deputy. Would you be interested? I could use a hardworking man who has a good head on his shoulders," said Jim.

"Are you serious?"

"I sure am. I think we could make a good team. I hope Babe will approve. What would you think about Tony being a lawman?"

"It's okay with me if this is what he wants to do. I'll go along with whatever he decides. I'm going outside to tend to the dogs. You two talk it over."

I returned in an hour. Much to my surprise, Tony and Jim were down on the front room floor reading a map of the lake. Tony had marked all the good cribs and fishing holes. They exchanged ideas. A special friendship had begun.

When I started dinner, Jim realized he needed to go home. It would soon be suppertime.

"It's getting late. I need to leave. I'll expect to hear of your decision in a couple of days," Jim said.

"Fine. You live close, so I'll stop in and let you know."

Jim waved goodbye and carefully trudged over the snow until he was out of sight.

"I've supported myself with carpentry work since I moved to Wisconsin. I like my work, but it would be nice to have a steady income. I want to give it a try. If it doesn't work, I can go back to what I do now," Tony said.

"True, you're good at what you put your mind to. There isn't anything you can't build, and I think you'll do excellent as a deputy too."

He accepted the position and looked forward to his new job with enthusiasm. Excited, we talked about the things we could do with a steady income.

Being gone for long hours would be part of the job. We would have to get used to a new routine.

"Let's save half of any money we have left after we've paid our bills. We could use the savings to pay for unexpected expenses and buy things we would like to have," Tony said.

"We'll be rich. I married you for your money," I teased.

Jim set up a work schedule. Tony trained ten hours a day. My daytime hours were filled with chores to do. Housekeeping kept me busy. When Tony worked nights, time dragged.

The instruction lasted six weeks. When he finished, he liked what he had learned and looked forward to his new position.

"I made the right decision to work for the county. Jim knows what he's doing. He's a good sheriff," Tony said.

"I'm glad for you. I'm darn proud of what you've done," I answered.

The relationship between Tony and Jim continued. Compatible, they were a perfect match.

CHAPTER 3

Hallelujah

Having no idea what it's like to witness winters change over to spring on a Northwoods lake, I squeamishly experienced it for the first time after Tony's graduation.

Excited and proud of his new job accomplishment, I wanted to celebrate and said, "Let's go out this weekend for dinner. We need to do something out of the ordinary. You graduated, and you're a deputy now."

"Why? Do you think this is special?"

"It is. You spent a lot of hours behind books and in the field."

"Let's stay here. Maybe you wouldn't mind broiling us a steak. It would be a lot cheaper," he said with his can't-say-no smile.

We both agreed to cook at home. This would be our salute to his new achievement.

While I washed the dishes, I heard a noise. It sounded like a loud moan. Without repeat, I disregarded it.

Later, I plunked close to the fireplace and worked on my cross-stitch project while Tony sat in his favorite chair and read the newspaper.

I heard the sound again and frowned. "Did you hear it?"

I ran to Tony's side. The noise repeated. Frightened, I said, "Maybe it's a bear or more than one animal!" I shivered.

I held on to Tony's shirt as though it were a tent to hide in and buried my head in his armpit.

Tony's strong arms around me brought comfort until he started to laugh. He couldn't help himself. I became defensive.

"Come on, Babe. It's the sound of ice breaking up on the lake. It makes all kinds of weird noises. Are you really afraid?"

"Don't you laugh at me! I never lived by a lake before. How did I know?" I scolded.

Tony walked over to the front door and opened it wide.

"Come over here and listen," he said.

I stood close to Tony. The sound gave me a chill at first. The more I listened, the less afraid I became.

      ～   ～   ～

During the next month, migrating birds returned, and pussy willows bloomed.

As the ice melts off the lakes, the fishing season opens. When the water is at its coldest, the action is at its peak.

Tony wanted to go out on the first day of fishing and asked Jim to join him. He wanted to show Jim his hidden cribs and holes. Both had a good catch and caught their limit.

"Tony, I wish you wouldn't fillet the fish close to the house. It stinks," I said.

"You're right. I'll fillet them someplace else."

A week later, he built a cleaning table close to the water.

"This will work better. We won't have the smell inside anymore."

"Did I ever tell you you're a smart fella?" I laughed.

The ground was still frozen in some places, causing big puddles to lay across the roads. The mud can be so thick it sucks up objects like quicksand.

Jim realized the sinking mud made a problem for Tony. Offering a solution, he said, "Instead of walking to work, why not drive in with me? You live close, and there's room in my car."

"It will be temporary. I can come over to your place, and you won't have to backtrack," answered Tony. Both agreed to give it a try.

By law, road limits go into effect when street conditions are unstable from the thaw. The limits were on.

Tree frogs started to sing round the clock, occasional bullfrogs croaked, wolves howled for their mates, and the buzz of humming-birds crossed our paths. Warmer days were here. The roads dried up, and the nasty black stuff disappeared.

Tony helped me put up a clothesline.

"Let me do it. I'm much taller than you," he said.

"Would you? It's hard for me to reach. Are you going to keep riding with Jim? When you walk, your clothes get splashed from the mud. They're a mess to wash."

"I'm going to continue to ride with him. The extra time we have for shoptalk is beneficial. You don't have to wash icky clothes anymore," Tony said.

"Hallelujah!"

CHAPTER 4

Nightmare

A loud clap of thunder took me by surprise. I jerked and jumped in response. Will I always react this way when I'm exposed to a close thunderstorm? In a split second, my mind took me back to a vicious lightning strike I barely recovered from.

The day had begun like any other. Tony found summer to be the best time of year to work on the house. With windows and doors open, pleasant breezes circulated.

Jim, now a close friend, helped us when he could. With trial and error, water from the well now pumped into our kitchen and bathroom. Walls had been torn down.

"Things are sure a mess around here. When will this house return to normal?" I complained.

"Don't worry," Tony said. "When we're done, I'll remove the plaster dust. There isn't much you can do in here, Babe, but you can work on the beach. I'll call you at four to start dinner."

"Okay. Do you need anything before I go?"

"Some more iced tea would be good, thanks."

I changed into my swimsuit in a flash, delivered the cold drink, and scurried to the lake.

I had started this beach project early in June with a rake and my bare hands. I cleared weeds from along the shoreline. It had been to my advantage that the weeds were sporadic and thin. In an organized manner, I moved from lakeshore to four-foot deep water. Back and forth, I cleared a section, about the width of the house. Near completion, I tackled one last large section of growth. I pulled the weeds as the sand beneath clouded. I waited for the water to clear when a creature attached itself to my thigh.

"Tony, help! Help me!" I screamed, lunging into a full run. "A leech is on my leg."

Tony didn't hear me. The ugly thing sucked my blood and made me shudder. We kept a salt shaker in the icehouse near the lake just for this purpose. A shake of salt dislodges its grip. With a solid dose of the white poison, the critter fell off. It wiggled its ugly self between the cracks of nearby rocks and disappeared.

My weed-clearing mission continued as dark clouds warned of danger. They rolled low and almost touched the ground.

"Get up to the house! Hurry! Get off the beach," Tony yelled.

Thunder clapped as lightning zapped through the threatening sky. Nothing could be done as a bolt of lightning directly hit the big old maple tree alongside our house. The wind-filled atmosphere spread the flames to our rooftop as we watched in terror. Our castle began to disappear before our eyes.

Neighbors close by gathered at our shoreline when sirens of the town's fire trucks wailed. They parked halfway between our lakeshore and the raging fire. Watchtowers had reported the smoke, and we watched as firefighters attached hoses and pumps into the lake. Water would be pumped to douse the flames. Heavy downpours provided the final punch to extinguish the determined and angry beast.

Numb, speechless, and heartbroken, we gazed motionless at the rubble. A dream—a horrible dream. It took a friend to shake us to reality. With our bodies and minds ready to crumble when our home dissolved, Jim said, "You two come on over to our place. We have plenty of room. You need time to decide how to handle things. We'll figure it out." A better friend we could never find.

"I don't know what to do or where to start," I said.

"At least we're safe. We'll rebuild somehow," Tony answered.

He took my hand and led me step-by-step to Jim's. I had met Jim's wife, Vera, only once. She greeted us with open arms.

"You two come right inside. Stay here as long as you need. I'm sorry the storm hit your place. Jim and I will do what we can to help you get back on your feet."

Feeling welcome, we hugged and thanked them.

When the storm subsided, only a few hours of daylight remained. Tony and Jim assessed the damage. Neighbors had remained at the site.

"We need to board things up," Jim suggested.

"There's not much left. A little remains around back where the kitchen stood."

"The neighbors will help," Jim assured.

"We'll help you put up a new place too. Don't worry," someone yelled.

Tony, filled with hope, returned with Jim. Vera served us a delicious fish dinner before showing us our beds.

"We appreciate this. We're exhausted," I said, hoping she could feel our gratitude.

"Jim and I have extra clothes. We're about the same size. Help yourselves. You can wash up and change when you're ready."

To find outfits and pajamas didn't take long. Our choices were many. Once we were cleaned up, we sat and discussed our options.

When our suntanned bodies collapsed in bed, our eyes closed, but sleep did not come. Visions of our home burning flashed before us.

"We're going to be all right," Tony reassuringly said.

I moved close to him and whispered, "The only thing important is we're both okay."

The door closed on our nightmare with newfound hope for the future.

CHAPTER 5

Congratulations

The next day, Tony and I went back to the rubble from our burnt house to gather salvageable items. The smell of charred wood and the sight of complete destruction overwhelmed me. I wept.

"I can hardly look at this. There is nothing to save."

"Yes, there is! See my screwdriver and hammer over there? They are covered with black soot, but if I remove the grime, they'll be usable again. Your stainless steel roasting pan is covered too. We can restore it back like new with a little elbow grease," Tony said.

Because he spoke positive, my tears vanished and I felt hopeful.

Mom and Dad invited us to move in with them until we rebuild. Salvaged items were stored in their garage. Our fire insurance provided enough money for us to pay off the mortgage on the burned house. Our precious land gave us the collateral to obtain a loan to build a new home.

Friends who lived around our lake and some in town volunteered to help with the construction. We had all the help we needed. Dad, Tony, Mom, and I penciled scratched plans for our new castle.

The debris from the fire knocked down easily. Large tractors scooped up the ugly charcoal-burnt garbage and dropped it into dump trucks. Three trucks were used and loaded one after another, paraded through town to the landfill. New materials to rebuild came from Mr. Powdy's general and hardware store. Items not in stock were ordered.

Tony, Dad, Jim, and Vera and I worked on the new house in our spare time. Community volunteers did the same.

Tony started cracking jokes and whistled. I talked about the choices for the outside structure and hummed a few tunes. Our spirits were lifted and we began to feel confident about having a place to call home again. Before the cold weather, our new building stood strong and complete.

In September, while fall colors peaked, we moved in. The aroma of new wood and fresh paint filled our new space. It seemed as though a fire had never taken place. With used furniture from friends and family, we had a kitchen table, four chairs, a double bed from Mom and Dad's, and two living room chairs.

Tony planned to build new furniture while I intended to sew curtains and draperies. A second chance to redecorate your entire home doesn't happen often. Joy replaced the pain of our loss. It evaporated like early morn's fog.

Yelling "Surprise!" our neighbors presented us with a housewarming party. Gifts were piled high on the counters and table. We laughed and cried. One guest brought his accordion and played polkas. Another brought beer. Women brought sandwiches, deserts, and coffee. The house filled with laughter and song while we enjoyed the accordion music. Wooden floors vibrated from dancing in our bare feet.

Our last guest left at 2:00 a.m. Tony and I looked at each other in amazement. At this moment, we were the only two people in the world. Him, me, and nobody else.

~ ~ ~

Snow came early in October as we celebrated our second Columbus Day anniversary. It felt good to be safely snuggled in our home again. We were content to sit by the fireplace to chat and embrace the kindness and generosity of the people who helped us.

While we sipped hot cocoa, we reminded each other how good life is despite its tragedies. Our friends and neighbors were people to love.

Winter always seemed long until we got close to the holidays. Tired as of late, I found myself sleeping more than usual, at times falling asleep while perched straight-up in a chair. Tony got up before me often. "Sleepyhead, it's about time you woke up," he teased.

Casually I shared my plight with my mother next time she visited.

"Mom, I am so tired. It isn't like me. Do you think something's wrong?"

She smiled, looked me right in the eye, and said, "Is it possible you might be pregnant?"

"It couldn't be. Oh! My gosh, Mom! It could be. Do women get so tired when they're pregnant?"

"It's normal. It will pass in a few weeks."

For the next few days, I found myself in a tither as I thought about motherhood. I didn't know much about babies. I wondered how Tony would take the news. We never talked about a family. He's Tony and I'm Babe. There isn't anyone else.

"Tony, I might be pregnant."

He looked at me, shocked, his eyes were as big as saucers. "Pregnant?"

After explaining my suspicions, he didn't say much and walked into the front room. He sat on the sofa and said, "Come here and sit by me." I sat close to him and looked into his blue eyes.

"Are you happy about the baby?" I asked.

"Happy? You're darn right I am. I want the best for you and the baby. Nowadays, babies are born in hospitals. I'd like this for you. When do you think it will be born?"

"In early June."

Tony seemed quiet for a few seconds as though he were deep in thought. He surprised me when he said we should have a car. Being speechless, I didn't say a word.

"Funds have come through from the state and a new county road will be built. It will go past our place and into town. With a family, we'll have plenty of need for a car. It's time for me to quit riding to work with Jim anyway. I need to be able to get you to the hospital on time. We won't need sleds or the buggy much after the road is in. What do you think? We have enough money to buy one," Tony said.

"Wonderful! Imagine going to town in a car. It will be nice with the baby. Usually electric services come in soon after a new road goes in. I can hardly wait," I answered.

Two weeks later, Tony came home with a 1929 model two-door sedan. Feeling excited, he wanted us to go for a ride. We stopped by Jim and Vera's house. Tony took Jim for a spin. Vera and I waited on their front porch.

"I wanted you to be the first person I tell. I think I'm pregnant. Tony and I are getting used to the idea," I said.

"You won't believe this. I just discovered I'm pregnant too." Overjoyed, we found ourselves in a spontaneous hug.

When the boys returned, the four of us had coffee and talked about the car and the new babies we would bring into this world.

"Congratulations, Jim," Tony said.

"Congratulations to the four of us."

CHAPTER 6

Survival

Desperate for income to feed their families and selves, men lined the city streets, waiting to apply for jobs. Times were frantic. In October of 1929, the banks had crashed, having no mercy on individuals whose complete financial security relied on the banking system. The economy had collapsed. Citizens were at the doorway of starvation.

Rural areas became less stressed with their ability to self-sustain off the land. We were among the fortunate. Even with the depression, Tony and I were happy as we entertained the idea of parenthood. Jim and Vera were due to become a mom and dad within days of our expected date. Our friendship took on new meaning. We were family.

Vera and I knew very little about babies. "Let's visit some of the mothers around the lake. Maybe they'll share some of their baby wisdom with us," Vera suggested.

"Okay." I giggled.

We laughed and joked about diaper changes, bottle sterilization, and how to manage baby laundry. The experienced moms made things look easy. Both of us became more confident.

When Mother visited, I bombarded her with questions. Being one of five children, I knew she'd have good advice.

"How do you know what to do when a baby cries a lot?" I asked.

"You worry too much. God knew what He was doing when He made mothers. Most everything will come naturally. You'll know by the sound of the cry what the baby needs."

"I hope you're right. I've started to gather things I know we'll need. I bought a diaper pail this week."

Jim and Tony were doing their dad thing. Father had old wind-up trains stored in his attic.

"They're not doing any good boxed up. Take them, Tony. You and Jim can make them like new. There's enough for both of you to put together trains and villages to use around your trees next Christmas. Babies like to watch the choo-choos go around," he laughed.

The fathers-to-be took on their new projects. The babies wouldn't see their displays for months. I wondered who the shiny tracks and miniature towns were really for.

The Great Depression knocked on every door. Tony came home from work with a frown on his face. While he squinted his eyes, he said in a soft voice, "Things are getting bad out there. I'm starting to worry about us."

Being naive, I didn't understand the magnitude of the disaster. "We'll be okay, right?" I asked.

"Don't worry, Babe. We can live off the land like everyone else around here. Most of our savings are gone because of the new car. We don't stand to lose a lot with the little bit of money we had in the bank. Hold supper for me a bit. I'm going to paint before dinner."

"Sure, we can wait."

I knew something upset him more than usual. Tony always painted when he was frustrated beyond his comfort zone.

The radio and newspapers reported sad stories about the Depression. People were frightened. Unable to get money from their banks, they didn't have enough cash on hand to buy food or pay their mortgages. Homes were being lost and countless small businesses went bankrupt. Unable to handle their devastation, many took their own lives. The Statue of Liberty shed tears. America suffered.

Tony worried about his job. Jim assured him he would still be needed.

"Your job will be more important than ever. Crime will increase as people become increasingly desperate. I can't see either one of us out of work. If we were, this country will be in serious trouble."

"Good. With the babies on their way, this would be a bad time to lose our jobs."

"We're going to be among the fortunate, Tony. We'll be okay," said Jim.

There were few jobs up north. The population is small and we were used to a simple lifestyle. Wild game, fish, and open fields were at our beckon call. We always had food and firewood to keep us warm.

In 1933, the government formed the Civilian Conservation Corps camps, known as the CCC. Set up across the USA, they allowed able-bodied men who wanted to work to have jobs. Together they built roads, bridges, and landscaped across the country. The CCC structures, much like our lumber camps, functioned well. Money earned helped families survive.

Men would stay at the camps during the week. If they lived close enough to go home, they left on weekends. Others stayed.

Jim had called it right. Crime rates rose. He and Tony were busier than normal and put in extra hours. Most calls were for drunk and disorderly complaints.

The money we had covered basic necessities. We harvested game and grew gardens. Having plenty of wood from the forests for fuel and ice from the winter's frozen lake for refrigeration, we were comfortable.

Most residents of the Northwoods owned their property by homestead. Tony had homesteaded when he first came to the Northwoods in 1923. We were secure landowners. This land arrangement had a free government program to help citizens of the USA obtain land of their own to build homes. One hundred sixty acres were given to each family for a small fee. The agreement being for the skilled pioneer to live on the given land for five years. When completed, a deed to ownership would be received. The act went into effect in 1862 and ended officially in 1976. In 1935, it greatly decreased when President Roosevelt set lands aside for government development.

~ ~ ~

Time dragged after the holidays. Vera and I were so-called "showing" and had lost our girlish figures completely.

"I'm tired of maternity clothes. There is no possible way I can hide this tummy bump anymore. I hope we can fit back in our clothes after the babies come," I complained.

"I'm finding it harder to get around. Are you?" Vera asked.

"A little bit. I tire easier than I usually do."

We waited for the snow to melt and the ice to break. Vera and I kept busy getting things ready for the little ones. Tony and Jim made beautiful cribs for the babies with leftover wood from our house. It seemed to Vera and me there was little our men couldn't do.

With extra CCC manpower, roads planned before the Depression were done as soon as spring road limits were lifted. The road that was planning to run past our house took shape late in the spring. We received notice from the power company that power lines were going up. Electricity would be hooked up within ten days. Telephone poles would be installed afterward. Two months later, four-party phone lines were installed in homes along roadside.

"Isn't this wonderful, Tony? I never thought we'd have power and phone service before the baby came. Did you?"

"I heard talk but didn't take it seriously. This is great. Now I will be able to keep in touch with you throughout the day. We won't have to mess around with the kerosene lamps anymore. We can use electric light. Life is getting so easy. Things sure do change."

"Do you think we can afford to buy those kind of lamps?" I asked.

"Yes, we have money left this month. Our power is hooked up. Let's go shopping and buy one," Tony answered.

We made a trip to town to see the new world of electric gimmicks and gadgets. Being new to us, all the choices looked good. I chose a plain white ceramic base table lamp. Tony had no objection. He selected a one-hundred-watt light bulb while I found a lampshade.

When we got back home, Tony hooked up this magnificent invention and placed it in the center of our table. Enchanted, we stood with our eyes glued on its beautiful glow. It lit the room from corner to corner. We had light for meals and reading anytime we chose. In the next six months, we were able to purchase three other lamps. Once used to the steady, even light, we didn't want to be without.

Telephone lines went up as planned. Town residents had electricity and phone hooked up for five years. Our line connection had four parties. When a call came through for one of us, all the phones rang in unison. We respected one another's privacy and politely hung up when the call came for someone else.

Mom and Dad had phone lines as well. Being able to stay in contact with my parents became a new luxury. With the baby due soon, I felt secure when I was home by myself.

"Now, don't forget, Babe, if anything starts to happen with the baby, you call me right away. Why don't you call your mom and ask her to come and stay with us a while? You're about due. I would feel better if you weren't home alone when I'm gone," Tony fretted.

"I'll be all right. Things are quiet. I'll call Mom anyway to ask her. Maybe Dad would bring her over. You go to work. Don't worry, I am fine. I'll call you later." We kissed goodbye and I watched Tony until out of sight.

The Depression raged on, but we were blessed and secure. There was no question in my mind that Tony, the baby, and I were fortunate survivors. Our family had a strong footing just as our nation had. We all survived from the pits of financial hell.

CHAPTER 7

Hello, David

D r. Arnold said to expect our precious arrival on June 13. My mother agreed to stay with us until delivery, giving Tony peace of mind. He worried about me being alone.

Vera and I continued to visit each other frequently. Our due dates were two weeks apart. While we visited, Vera said, "Wouldn't it be a hoot if we delivered on the same day?"

"It would be too accidental if our babies had the same birthday. The hospital only has two beds in the maternity ward. We'd be in the same room. I'm a little excited about having our baby in the hospital. Are you?" I answered, half laughing.

After she left, I sat on the front porch and watched a bird buzz back and forth. Something warm ran down my leg. Did the pressure from the baby on my bladder cause an accident? I had no clue.

Embarrassed, I didn't tell Mom. As the afternoon progressed, I cramped. The discomfort turned into pain and intensified. Mom heard my moans.

"Oh my goodness. How long have you felt like this? The baby will be here soon."

Mom took over and decided to call the doctor and Tony, but the phone required nickels to be inserted in a slotted box to reach the phone operator. Once connected, she would say, "Number please" and proceed to make the connection. Neither Mom nor I had any nickels.

"Tony has slugs on his workbench. Use them," I groaned. These plain pieces of gray-colored metal were the same size as a nickel and could be used in place of a real coin. The phone collector came monthly to empty the box. We had to replace real money for the slugs to pay our bill.

As the pain increased, so did my groans. "Oh my god! Do something. I can't stand it."

"I found the slugs!"

"It hurts so bad. Hurry up."

"Take deep breaths. I talked to the doctor. She's on her way. We'll do the best we can. Tony's on special detail. I can't reach him."

Dr. Arnold arrived within the hour. She and Mom did an amazing job delivering our healthy eight-pound boy. His first squeaky cries turned my anguish into joy.

Mom gently cleaned and oiled his pink baby flesh and wrapped him in a flannel blanket. He smelled sweet and fresh, ready to meet his daddy. When placed in my arms, he knew me. His cry stopped. He stared at me with sparkling eyes when he heard my voice. To my surprise, his coloring matched mine. Brown hair circled his face.

"What are you going to name him?" Mom asked.

"I'm not sure. Tony and I will decide together. I like David. Do you think he looks like a David?"

Dr. Arnold gathered her instruments to leave and said, "He does look like a David. Nice name for a handsome boy. Call me if you have any problems. I'll see you in about six weeks."

~　～　～

Word traveled to Tony's office, announcing the arrival of federal agents. Multiple arrests were anticipated. A local resort owner had heard rumors that Finellie, a well-known criminal, and his gang were in the Northwoods. The situation meant the sheriff and his deputies would be called to assist, but at the time, he did not expect to be involved.

Finellie and four additional well-dressed male guests with their lady friends appeared at his registry desk. He knew instantly who they were. The guns they carried could be seen bulging under their suit coats. Secretly, the owner telephoned for help—the message was to be forwarded to the FBI.

Within two hours, the resort grounds were covered in law officers and my Tony! Long after dark, Finellie got word the FBI knew his location. A wild shoot-out started and the culprits escaped from a resort window in the main house. Two agents were shot and Tony's right shoulder grazed. A crazy dangerous car chase followed. The fugitives escaped. The cause lost.

In the wee hours of the morning, Tony came home. I greeted him with deep concern for his injury. The disappointment of the sheriff's department's defeat became short-lived and healed with the introduction of his precious son.

Tony held me close and said, "Oh my god, Babe, I didn't know. I feel bad I wasn't here with you. Are you okay?"

"Look, Tony, isn't he a beautiful baby?" I asked as I opened the blanket to expose his perfect feet and toes. "What should we call him? I love the name David. Can we call him David?"

Tony smiled. "Hello, David," he said with his blue eyes twinkling like they always do when he's pleased.

~ ~ ~

Tony had two weeks off work because of his injury. With him home to help, Mom returned home. David's first two weeks of life were spent with Tony and me.

No longer Tony, me, and nobody else; we were Tony, me, a family of three.

CHAPTER 8

Premonition

Jim and Vera's son James entered the world six days after David's birth. Our babies kept us close in touch. It seemed natural to spend the upcoming Fourth of July holiday together. The four of us decided to picnic on Jim and Vera's patio.

Abruptly, we wasted no time in pushing our babies' buggies up close to the house. Grabbing the boys, we took shelter inside. An inquisitive skunk watched us scramble with a smile on his face. We needed to get away from the critter, right now! We made it on time.

Contentment, joy, and pride had become ours. As new families, we savored every day as something special. This is who we were now. Little James had a crown of rust-colored hair. David had chestnut. When we were together their coloring difference made it easy to tell them apart. Vera and I gave the boys nicknames.

"Let's call James 'Rusty.' It suits him," said Vera.

"Okay. We can call David 'Sport.' This is what Tony calls him most of the time anyway," I suggested. Vera agreed.

While we were waiting for Mister Skunk to leave, Tony said, "We need to build a dock and get a boat. When Sport is big enough, we'll be able to fish together."

I smiled. David couldn't walk yet, and his father believes his son needed a boat and a dock. No doubt he adored our little boy.

When the nasty visitor left, Jim and Tony cooked our meal on an outside pit. We ate on blankets we had spread out near the beach. Meanwhile our little ones slept nearby in their buggies. Vera and I took turns checking on them while our husbands casted for fish. Jim hooked into a big old turtle. "Soup! Let's make turtle soup! I hear it's good eaten," he yelled.

Vera's eyebrows raised. A frown crossed her face. Turtle soup wasn't in her vocabulary. "Not me, I don't do turtle soups!"

Just then another black-and-white furry critter had strolled down the deer path. It stopped the soup discussion.

"Skunk! What's this nasty thing doing here? Maybe we should make skunk soup." Vera laughed.

None of us wanted to aggravate this visitor. Jim let the turtle go, and we retreated to the house, hoping "Stinky" would leave. He stayed long enough to cast a horrible odor. You could detect it a mile away.

Before we left, Tony and Jim talked about the boat dock. "We have lumber and nails left from the house. Do we need treated wood for under the water?" Tony asked.

"Treated works better than regular wood but it's still wood. Why don't we use pipe for under water and treated wood for the dock?"

"Good idea. We'll make use of what's lying around too," said Tony.

The creative geniuses found all the material needed for the dock. In three weeks, it stood strong and grand. The rest of the summer, we dangled our bare feet in the cool water while we sat on the dock. The lake breeze cooled us in the summer's heat. We wondered how we ever got by without a dock.

As luck would have it, Tony spotted an old deserted row boat in the weeds of a nearby bay. He asked neighbors if anyone wanted to claim this piece of junk. When no one came forward, Tony rescued the craft with intentions to repair and refinish it. Once completed, a friend gave him a set of unused oars.

Truly happy, Tony whistled. Having his own fishing boat made another dream come true. There wasn't enough free time during the week for Tony to use the boat as much as he liked. I watched him from the kitchen window at sunsets as he circled the shoreline for walleye. A good catch always completed his day.

Fall came with changing colors throughout the forest. Leaves in vibrant yellows, oranges, and reds captured our breaths. When reflected off the water, the woods mirrored a piece of heaven.

Warm September days allowed me to hang laundry outdoors with David close by in his carriage. As I hung sheets, a strong wind current rushed through the trees. I wrestled with the bedsheets. They spun like a tornado. I turned to double pin a section of line.

Suddenly, my heart sank to my ankles and I gasped in horror! Terrified! Terrified…and furious! A large black bear stood alongside David's carriage. How dare he! I shrieked madly, throwing dripping sheets at the beast.

"GET AWAY! GET OUT OF HERE!" I screamed hysterically. Throwing wet laundry in his face, I gave no consideration to my safety. I surprised myself—both brave and bold.

Scared beyond his little world, David cried nonstop. The bear looked me square on, dropped on all fours, and waddled away. Ripples of fat wobbled on his back as he ran. Only then did I realize how huge he was. Still scared out of my wits, I grabbed David, clutched him to my bosom, and ran to the house.

Later, Tony said, "Bears only come around to investigate something of interest. Their noses lead them to food. We didn't leave any garbage around, did we? Maybe it caught the scent of the fish scrapes I buried by the lake. I'll check it out."

When Tony returned, he said raccoons had scattered the fish debris everywhere. "You know, Babe, bears are more frightened of you than you are of them unless you pose a threat to their cubs. You were pretty spunky for an old gal," he jested.

"What do you mean, 'old gal'? I wasn't afraid for a minute."

"Okay then, you're a tough old bird."

Stuffing a dinner napkin in his mouth crossed my mind. We chased around the kitchen while Sport watched his laughing parents from his high chair. When the pursuit finished, Tony grabbed me.

"What would you think if I decided to go to Canada this fall for five days to hunt ducks? If you don't want to stay here alone, you could stay with your folks in town."

"I guess you can go if you behave yourself." I giggled. "I'll just stay home alone while you have fun." I pouted with a pretend frown on my face. "Everything I need for David is here. It's much easier for me. I don't want to go to town. We have a phone and I can call if I need help. Jim and Vera are right next door too."

"I planned to ask Jim if he wanted to go with me. Do you think Vera will mind?"

"She would be all right with it. Besides, it might be fun for us girls to have time together. With everyone underfoot and interruptions, we don't have time for projects. I've wanted to make curtains for months, but I never have enough time."

Vera approved. The big boys would duck hunt in Canada. Another lifetime adventure awaited them. Excited, they were chatty and somewhat noisy as they packed their gear. Rope, a machete, burlap bags, double-barrel shotguns, ammunition, hip boots, old khaki wool army blankets, pot and pans, and who knows what all. With a heavy packed car, they were ready to roll. Their time for arrival would coincide with Canada's duck season.

"We'll bring back our limit and you'll have a good supply of down to make something," Tony said as he kissed me goodbye.

"Wonderful. We could use new soft pillows."

Vera and I watched them back out of the drive. We lingered until they were out of sight. We'd miss them but looked forward to extra project time.

Sleep escaped me the first two nights after they left. Unusual, I had no reason to be restless and wondered if it could be a premonition of danger ahead. What might the hunters encounter?

CHAPTER 9

The Nattily Marsh

Tony and Jim took turns driving almost nonstop to reach the marsh. While Tony had the wheel, he drove around a sharp curve. The windshield became black. With instinct, Tony used all of his strength to hit the brakes. Sharp swerves pulled the car from one side to the other. Jim braced himself against the dashboard. They came to a stop in a ditch.

"It's a moose! Look at the monster! It's so big it blacked out the windshield. The weeds hung down from its mouth and are on the window, only missed it by a couple of feet. It's bigger than the car. You drive for a while. I'm shook up," Tony said.

"Okay, it scared the s——t out of me too. Before we go, let's take a break. I need a drink of water." Recuperated, they left.

When they arrived at the resort, they were close to the "Nattily" marshes. Their cabin stood among trees close to the lake. In the silence around them, you could hear the leaves fall from the trees. Jim and Tony were the only hunters there.

"Tomorrow's weather is supposed to be perfect to duck hunt. Stormy, windy, and cold. This will bring them down. Let's be ready. We can load some of our gear in the boat tonight and get off to an early start tomorrow," suggested Jim.

"I'm tired, but it's a good idea. Once we're done, let's hit the sack early. I can set the alarm for 4:30 a.m. so we can get up on time."

Together they loaded their camouflage and shotgun supplies into the rented vessel. They arrived at the marsh with the first break of dawn. The north winds picked up. A definite pathway through the north end of the habitat showed through the shallow current. Dangerous rapid waters were at the opposite end of the marsh.

"I'll follow the path through the north end. Looks like a good place to set up. It's perfect. See all the water grass, cattails, and weeds? We could camouflage out of sight. The wind is really rippin'. Let's hunt here," Tony said. When set up, the hunt began.

While flying overhead, a steady stream of noisy ducks circled and glided across the marshes. Well hidden, the shots seemed to come out of nowhere. The hunters met the limits early. Both Tony and Jim were ecstatic. In their hip boots, they stepped with caution and walked from place to place to pick up their game. It didn't take long to pack up and return.

When they arrived at their dock, Canadian-native Indians greeted them. Their stern faces and brown eyes stared intensely. Long, black, uncombed hair draped over the shoulders of their unkempt clothes. Outreached arms and hands signaled back and forth from their mouths and stomachs to send their message of hunger. They were begging.

"Let's give them our ducks. It should be blustery for a couple of days. We can take our chances on a good hunt tomorrow," said Tony.

"Okay, fine with me. I never saw anyone beg like this before. Did you?"

"Only by the grace of God it's not us. Give them everything. We can make up for it before we go home. There is plenty of time," Tony said.

The next few days were duplicates of the first-day hunt. On the final day, the hunters went out with great expectation. Weather conditions changed. Midmorning brought a slow shift in winds as they changed to the south. Fewer ducks came in over the marsh at a slower pace.

"Don't think we're going to get our limit today. Let's pick up the few we have and head out. The water is getting deeper anyway," said Jim.

"We might as well. Not much action. Think we have about a dozen mallards between us."

Routinely, they brought their bounty to the boat. Jim lagged behind when he started to feel his boots squeeze him down.

"Oh my god! I'm in some kind of quicksand. I'm stuck, can't move. For God's sake, help me! Help me get out of here! I don't know if I can make it. I'm being sucked into the marsh. Hurry! Hurry up!"

"Don't fight it! Try not to move. Can you grab onto any tall grass or weeds? Hang on, I'll get something for you to grab."

Tony retrieved his machete from the boat, scrambled to the tall cattails, and swung with amazing speed. He assembled the strong weeds into a woven-style matt and, with precision, threw it out to Jim.

"Hang on to the matt, it will help you float. I'm throwing a rope too. Hang on to it and I'll pull you out."

"Pull hard! I'm cemented in these boots. Hurry up! The —— water is up to my neck!" Jim yelled. "Start praying."

With perfect aim, Tony pitched the rope exactly on target. Jim reached it and clutched onto it for dear life. The struggle to pull strong enough began as Tony's feet dug into muck. He strained every muscle in his body to pull his buddy to safety. Slowly, the suction surrounding the boots broke, releasing Jim. Tony continued to pull his friend up and over the weeds to sturdy ground.

Scratched, bruised, and bleeding with the shivers, Jim needed Tony's help to walk. The Canadian Indians came forward to help bring him inside. They were compassionate toward the hunters who had shared their game.

"I'll be glad to get home. The hunt here is good but the marsh is treacherous. I didn't realize the water depth and flow is controlled by the wind direction. Our spot isn't safe when the winds change. Next duck season, I'm not coming back. I'll hunt close to home," Jim said.

"I'm all for it. It's a miracle you got out alive. The Canadians can have the Nattily marshes. I'll settle for ours."

CHAPTER 10

Little John

I felt like a silly school girl with a crush. I went to the dresser mirror to check my appearance. Makeup and hairstyle were of utmost importance. Primped to my satisfaction, the wait began. Time dragged. I watched the hands of the clock move to late afternoon. Tony had called to tell me he and Jim were close to home and should be home by dinnertime, if not sooner. David and I made countless trips to the front window.

"Daddy will be home soon."

I opened the door before Tony got up the first step. His smile and open arms became an embrace. With closed eyes, my nostrils recognized Tony's special smell and I melted into his strong arms.

"I missed you. David did too. He looked for you and called 'Daddy' when he woke up from his naps."

"Honey, I'm glad to be back. You and David are my life. I love you," he whispered.

We played with David while we unpacked gear. After dinner Tony told me detail after detail of their horrific trip. "I can't believe you ran into so much trouble. Thank God you're both home safe. Please don't go back there again."

"We decided we'll hunt ducks here next season. Doubt we'll ever go back again."

"Good, you'll get just as many here," I answered.

"One of these days when David is older, I'm going to take him with me. Then you'll have twice the feathers and down for pillows," laughed Tony.

"Guess I'll have to wait awhile," I teased back.

~ ~ ~

Winter arrived. As we anticipated David's first Christmas, Daddy made sure a train ran around our tree. Preparing for the holidays wore me out. There were so many things to do in a short period of time. When David took his afternoon naps, I laid down beside him and fell asleep too.

This isn't like me. Am I lazy? How could I be tired midday? Am I pregnant? When I carried David, I remember being tired the first few months. Oh my god! The calendar tells it all. Yes! I might be.

I chose not to tell Tony until I saw Dr. Arnold. I'd see her soon with David's checkup.

After examination, with a smile on her face, she told me, "Congratulations, Beatrice! We can expect this baby next August."

Our little boy had brought us so much joy. Two times the love would be incredible.

Tony picked us up at the doctor's office. I decided to tell him.

"How would you feel if we were to have another baby?"

"Pretty darn good. Why wouldn't I? Are you pregnant?" he asked with wide-eyed excitement.

"I am. Dr. Arnold just gave me a physical. She said I'm due in August. Vera is due in June. Here we go again," I laughed.

We talked about the new baby and what our plans should be. David could see how happy we were, and he babbled along with us. Life was good.

~ ~ ~

Tony and I awoke at 3:00 a.m. by a loud thump and bang on our front door. As I sat up in bed, I reached to turn on the lamp. Tony jumped to his feet and put on his trousers.

"Stay in the bedroom. I'll see who it is. Who would come in the middle of the night?" he said.

Voices entered my reality. I heard Jim and Vera. I ran downstairs. Their painful faces and tired eyes terrified me. Vera trembled as she threw her arms around me, barely able to speak, and told me, "Rusty's dead! Rusty's gone! My baby's gone! Why? Why did God take him away? I hate Him!"

"He turned cold and blue! We found him in his crib! I drove to the hospital to try and save him but too much time had gone by. Crib death, they said. I can't believe it. He's so little," echoed Jim.

"God didn't do this. He loves the three of you. You know He walks with you always. Rusty is loved and cradled in Jesus's arms," I struggled to say.

"You think so? My baby has to be all right," said Vera.

While I comforted her, Tony eased Jim's pain and sat alongside him on the couch. He offered a handkerchief and said, "I'm so sorry! You will get through this. Babe and I will help you."

Tony and I pulled ourselves together as Jim and Vera were beyond reason. Tony put on a pot of coffee. We went into the kitchen.

"When did you eat last?" I questioned.

"Dinner last night," Jim said.

"Drink some juice or coffee. Have some freshly baked Kugan."

"I'm not hungry. I don't ever want to eat again," Vera cried.

"You need to eat for the little one inside you. Try to nibble at least," I begged.

With hesitance, she managed to eat a small amount. Jim followed. We talked until dawn. We needed to call our pastor and we did.

Once he arrived, the pastor stayed close to Vera and Jim's side. The arrangements were made for Rusty to be waked at home and buried in the town cemetery.

Vera and Jim needed to rest. Tony drove them home. When David woke up, I held him close and bowed my head in thankfulness. I wondered if seeing David would upset Vera. How would she feel around another baby? And how does she feel about the child she carries?

Early the next day, Vera found refuge at our house. Still in shock, she couldn't help Jim to make calls to notify family or make any decisions. Tony helped in her place. Jim made the calls while Tony put a black wreath on their front door. He pushed furniture back to the walls in their living room to make room for the wake.

With the funeral director's help, Rusty's body was laid to rest in a little white satin-lined cherrywood casket. A sturdy stand held everything in place against the wall at one end of the living room. Two white floral pieces, symbols of purity and innocence, were placed at each end of the casket. The casket cover remained closed until Jim and Vera were able to make the first view of Rusty.

With furniture pushed back, rows of chairs were placed in the middle of the room for friends and family to visit and attend service. When the final details were taken care of, Tony brought Jim back to our house to get Vera.

"Honey, we have to go back home now. It's time for us to be there for Rusty. Your mom and dad are on their way. Everything is ready for our guests," said Jim.

"I don't know if I can do it. I don't know," cried Vera.

"We'll go with you. You can do it. You want things to be nice for Rusty, don't you?" I asked.

"I'll try. I really will. Bring David with you."

Vera appeared to be glad to see David. Holding out her arms to hold him, she said, "Come here, sweetheart, give Vera a hug."

Greatly relieved, I placed Sport in her arms.

We gathered together in front of the casket when it was opened. Vera wailed at the first sight of Rusty. She touched him and wanted to pick him up. Jim held her to steady her on her feet. Tears streamed down his cheeks. "You can't pick him up, honey. It's going to be all right. Rusty is in Jesus's arms. This is only his earthly body."

Together they sat down in the front row of chairs, held each other, and wept. Tony and I were unable to hold back the tears. Our dearest friends were in so much pain.

Neighbors began to arrive. The distraction helped Vera and Jim compose themselves. During the next two days, Tony and I stayed with Vera and Jim as much as possible. Friends and neighbors came out in large numbers. At times, the receiving line reached through the house and out the front door. Baked goods and casseroles were brought by thoughtful friends and served in the kitchen. Their home had temporarily lost its joy and was replaced with an outpouring of love from all of the dear people who shared their grief.

The day of the funeral, the sight of Rusty's casket ready to be put in the ground overwhelmed Vera. It crushed her spirit. Her knees buckled as she fainted into Jim's arms. Being a strong man, he kept her from falling. With deep sadness in his heart, he tenderly carried her to the car.

Unable to go back to the gravesite, I offered to stay with her. Jim went back to his son's funeral. Tony stayed with him until the service ended.

Vera and Jim grieved the loss of their son. Being at work every day seemed to distract Jim. Vera could not sleep, and it showed. She had deep circles under her eyes. To come to our house for the day calmed her fears. She stayed until Jim returned home in the evenings.

With their baby soon due, I thought it might help Vera to emphasize the needs of the new little one.

"I can help you bring down the small clothes you stored away in the attic. I might have some extra receiving blankets never used by David. Would you like them?" I asked.

"You better hang on to them yourself. Don't forget, you're pregnant too." We both laughed. Putting my hand on my baby bump, I said, "How could I forget?"

To focus on the needs of the new life-to-be seemed to help Vera. The rocking cradle freshened with new linens, baby bottles and nipples sterilized, and all the tiny clothes neatly stacked, they were ready for a visit from the stork.

Pastor Bill continued to stop by often to visit them. Being a man of great faith, he brought comfort. You could see the look of peace on their faces after his visits.

June arrived. Almost to the day expected, Vera gave birth to a healthy eight-pound baby boy, his hair rust in color like Rusty's. They wept tears of joy when they welcomed little John.

The pain of losing Rusty would always be a special memory in our hearts forever.

CHAPTER 11

Partners with Pride

Completely fascinated, I watched car after car drive past our front yard. The sound of the tires hummed a new song that was foreign to me. Where did the endless quiet go? Sounds of the loon calling across the lake were often muffled out.

Warm days of summer had brought vacationers to the Northwoods. The county's new road to town ran past our property, inviting people to take advantage of the new shortcut. Travelers looked for gas, food, and rest. Residents, including us, were stopped and questioned about locations of services. The needs became obvious.

Tony called me to join him. "Come sit by me. I want to talk to you about an idea I have. We need a gas station here. There is a long stretch from our town to Eagle River with no gas available. The depression is over, and the economy is strong again. I talked with a district manager from Standard Oil, and he is very interested in the idea and told me a bank is going to open in town this summer.

"The Carters remodeled their place and opened a restaurant two blocks away. Sometimes they have more business than they can handle. I want to take a chance and leave my deputy job to go into the gas station business. What do you think?"

"How would Jim feel if you left? And do we have enough money to buy a business?" I answered.

"I think so. A Standard Oil representative offered me a franchise. I would rather own the building. It would be more profitable, but this is all they will agree to. Later, when we're established, we can purchase one. Jim told me he is not running for sheriff next election. He might want to partner with me. We could run the business together. Our boys are getting bigger and they could be a great help. Between Jim and I, there would be enough money to get things started."

"It's true, our area has grown a lot over the past ten years, but so has our family. We have four mouths to feed now and so does Jim. Should we chance it?" I questioned.

"We can't afford not to."

"I trust your judgment. I'm game. See what Jim and Vera think."

Much to my surprise, they were receptive to the idea. Jim knew he wanted to leave the sheriff's office and hadn't decided what he would do to take its place.

"Good idea! We both live close to where the station would be. The snow toboggans are a favorite with tourists. We are used to the machines from our county job, so we know how to repair them and do general work on cars. No licenses are required. A repair shop for sleds and cars could be added income with what we would earn from the gas pumps. That addition would keep us busy enough to support two families. Let's do it! I believe it will work," Jim answered with a grin from here to Alaska.

～　　～　　～

Jim and Tony left the sheriff's office on a sad note. The people they worked with had become their friends They would be missed. Living close by, perhaps they could keep in touch.

Well-qualified, the new sheriff picked up on his new responsibilities with ease. Tony and Jim were able to leave the job with no concerns, putting into motion the plan that had been agreed upon by everyone concerned.

Tony handled the purchase of the station while Jim organized the equipment. With perfect timing, the new bank opened. We obtained a business loan with them. Their encouragement gave us a sense of community.

The four of us joked a lot and talked about things we wanted to buy if we earned enough money. Happy dispositions and enthusiasm filled our every thought. None of us allowed ourselves to think about the debt required. If we had not had the four of us, we would have been scared out of our wits.

Contracts concerning the station were completed. The name JT's Standard became the official agreed-upon name. Ready and able, the men opened their business with anticipation.

Our new means of support boomed from the first day we opened. In the fall, when the children went back to school, the demand from vacationers dropped off. By some miracle, we had picked up enough local business to survive. We were the only repair shop within eighty miles.

Tony took time off to surprise me. "I want you to come with me to Mr. Powdy's to look at something."

"Look at what?" I questioned.

"You'll see when we get there."

My cheeks were flushed with excitement. He led me to the back of the store, smiled, and said, "You've waited a long time for a good machine to do laundry. There is a lot of laundry for six of us. If we don't get it now while we have the money, I don't know how long you will have to wait."

"We really do need it. I know just the one I'd like to have. The tub and wringer are extra big. I'd be done with laundry in no time with one this size," I answered. I softly smiled with excitement while I compared models.

We placed an order and returned home. I watched the calendar for delivery day. I added separated piles of laundry and envisioned myself putting super-sized loads through the wringer.

The day finally came. What a wonderful playtime I had. I completed the laundry in half of the time I used to before the glorious machine became part of our household.

⁓   ⁓   ⁓

When the snow arrived, we purchased a tow truck and snow plow attachment. Well-used, it plowed the station driveways and answered requests for private driveway snow removal. Used after every winter storm, it provided unexpected income.

There were four gas pumps on our driveway with a front office directly inside the front door of the building. Displays of oil, tires, and batteries filled the space. Two pits with ladders were in the back room for oil changes and car repair. A designated space for snow machine jobs in one corner worked well. Two restrooms were on an outside wall. Vera and I shared the job to maintain them. We also did bookwork and prepared bank deposits.

The toboggans became known as snowmobiles. Quick to gain popularity, they became the number one winter sport of the north. It became necessary to expand the repair space at the station.

The first year, we had a bitter-cold winter. Automobiles broke down often with subzero temperatures. Tony and Jim worked hard. Their reputation for excellent work became well-known. Bringing sled repairs to them became a "must do" from most of their customers. We were the only auto shop with repair and tow truck in our area.

Tony and Jim were so busy on our first Christmas Eve as station owners that they had to sneak out the back door to make it home in time for the church service.

Because we were young and still felt indestructible, the men handled the stress with ease. The load they carried didn't faze them. Our plan worked well and we found ourselves rewarded.

Once established, our three sons, David, Bobby, and Anthony, were old enough to be a help. Jim's oldest son, John, joined them. They came in after school to take turns at the pumps and finished small jobs. We were definitely a family-owned and operated business.

Our daughter Clare, now fifteen, had a waitress job at Carter's restaurant in town. We were amazed by her ambition.

Beth, our youngest child, joined the family three years ago. We were surprised and delighted. The older children thought of her as a novelty. With fair skin and deep blue eyes like Tony, it's no wonder he called her his "baby girl."

With pride in their accomplishment, the two partners enjoyed their new lifestyle. Life became an enjoyable challenge for all of us.

CHAPTER 12

Animal Canyon

"The boys didn't show at the station after school. Are they home?"

"No, they're not here," I said. "Strange. Wonder what's going on? Hang up and I'll call the school to find out if they left at three o'clock. I'll call you back."

"Okay. Don't forget. Johnny didn't come in either."

Four o'clock, and no one answered at the school. I called Tony. Together we drove to places they might be and asked their friends if they had seen them. A basketball group played close to the school. We asked them, "Have you boys seen Jr., Bobby, or Johnny anywhere since school let out?"

"Saw them head toward the lake. Don't know where they were headed."

"Thanks. If you see them again, tell them we're looking for them and they should go to the station."

We lost an hour's time in our search. Still without leads, we were concerned.

"It won't be long before dark," I said. With a worried frown, I grabbed Tony's arm.

"Yep, it doesn't look good. This isn't like their usual pranks. We better search the woods and lake. Let's start where they were last seen."

Jim and four friends joined the investigative hunt. Tony suggested they bring rifles. The fall trees with vivid yellow leaves reflected the sun and brightened the shadowy forest.

"Let's not drive," Jim said. "We have a better chance of finding them on foot." The seven of us spread half a block apart, separated, and headed through the brush toward the water.

"Johnny! Bobby! Anthony!" we yelled.

A mile in, a large stressed animal roared. Tony's eyes met mine. Fear flooded my soul. I pictured the boys threatened by an enraged beast.

"Babe, you better go to the car. The rest of you, come with me. Follow the sound!" ordered Tony.

I started toward the car and froze. The more I moved, the louder the ferocious growl was. Before I regained my senses, a band of wolves circled and stared me down. Sharp jagged teeth snarled. Their drooling mouths spoke attack. I screamed, "Tony! TONY!"

The search party had heard the wolves' angry growls and moved swiftly toward the sound. They fired their guns. The wolves ran. I shook from my head to my feet. Fright overtook me.

"It's okay. They're gone. It's okay," Tony assured me. His arms comforted me.

"I don't want to go back. Tony, please let me stay with you."

"All right, stay close."

The men reloaded their rifles. We continued toward a magnified howl and found a fat full-grown black bear on the sandy water's edge. Its front paws firmly wrapped around an enormous fish. A bald eagle swooped the bear's head. The bird's screech was so shrill it pierced our ears.

We watched as the wolves returned for a battle of supremacy. The scene unfolded like a murder mystery—beyond our imagination. The boys! The boys! There! All three squeezed in a tree stand built for two. They sat on top one another with limbs flapping in all directions. How they squeezed into a two-man gear is beyond belief.

"Mom, Dad! Over here!"

We waved in response. Tony and Jim shot their rifles. The hungry pack of wolves ran, and the black furry bear, still dazed from the circling bird, dropped to all fours and trotted away. The noisy bird quieted and perched in a tree close to the fleshy fish. It waited for us to leave to enjoy his promised prey.

Tony yelled to the boys, "You can come down now. It's safe. Take your time so you don't knock one another over."

Unscrambling their arms and legs, they tumbled out of their shelter as I breathed sighs of relief. All safe! After a few motherly hugs, the terrified boys all spoke at the same time. Each unfolded their story.

"Dad, I thought the bear would eat us."

"We didn't have any place to go. My heart stuck in my throat."

"I ran for my life. Saw the tree stand. It seemed a mile away."

"We ran for cover! So fast I almost tripped!"

"We darted through the woods so fast. I don't think the black thing or the bird noticed. I figured we were goners!"

"Yeah, we beat him though. We were really fast."

The boys stood close to Tony and Jim, seeking approval for finding the hunters' perch.

"Not so fast, guys. What were you doing in the woods in the first place? You're supposed to come to the station right from school," scolded Tony.

"This ought to teach you one mighty lesson," echoed Jim.

The young men's heads dropped. Their fathers spoke truth. Another word was not to be spoken. We thanked our friends who had been glad to help. "The most important thing is everyone's safe," they said.

Deafening silence prevailed on the way home. During dinner, the children apologized. "We're sorry we went to the canyon and didn't tell you."

"Okay. But don't let this happen again," Tony said.

When the family retired for the night, Tony chuckled behind closed doors. "During my teens, I did a lot worse than running off to Animal Canyon."

"I'll bet you did!"

CHAPTER 13

The Family Gift

Half dazed at the break of dawn, Tony and the boys stumbled into the kitchen. Nobody said a word. Plunking down into their seats at the breakfast table, they slowly began to wake up. The excitement began.

"Did you hear those shots?" Bobby asked.

"Yeah, I did. We better finish up here and head out. You can each carry your own gun. You know the safety rules," Tony said.

"More shots! They're close to the house," Anthony added.

"Dad, look over by the icehouse. Looks like blood in the snow. Someone hunted in our yard," David announced.

"Shooting this close to a house is against the law. Whoever it is doesn't play by the rules. It's dangerous," Tony answered.

The pace of their conversation picked up as their faces reflected the excitement and thrill of opening day of shotgun deer season.

"We're going to hunt in Three Lakes today. You all know the rules and I expect you to follow them," Tony instructed.

Hunting for deer was important. If the hunt goes well, 50 percent of our years' meat is harvested. Our schools close, allowing families to hunt together.

With full stomachs, bundled warm from head to toe, and carefully carrying their guns, Tony and the boys left for the chase with great expectations. Between them, they brought home one buck and two does. Enough meat for the year.

As a family, we butchered and securely packaged the fresh meat. Each container was to be stored in the icehouse until needed. Tony made sausage we traditionally enjoy on New Year's Eve.

The fall came in unseasonably warm. Christmas was but a month away and we barely had a foot of snow on the ground. The weather so mild it didn't seem like the holidays. One day, while we made festive plans, Mom reminded me of an old wives' tale she grew up with: "A warm Christmas fills the cemetery."

"You don't really believe this, do you?" I asked.

"I don't know. I've heard this for as long as I can remember." We laughed and continued with our plans. Mom and Dad would join us for Christmas Eve dinner and church service then come back to our house to stay for the sabbatical week. We all looked forward to their visit.

On Sunday, December 7, 1941, while we were readying for church, I heard a news flash interrupting the morning radio program.

"I have reports of an attack on the United States. Moments ago, Japanese bombers attacked our US Naval Base at Pearl Island," the announcer reported. How could this be? US troops are fighting with allies in Europe against the German Nazis.

"Did you hear the report, Tony?" I questioned as I scurried from task to task.

"What report?"

"I heard an announcement saying the United States is engaged in battle, we were attacked by Japan. Come on, everybody, it's time leave." We left without further discussion.

Conversation among the men at church clarified the mixed reports on the radio. When we returned home, Tony tuned into the radio console in our living room. We heard a confirmation given by the network we always listened to.

Japan bombed Pearl Harbor in an attempt to wipe out the United States aircraft carriers. They thought the planes were docked there. Our battleships were assembled at this location while the carriers were elsewhere. The ships were badly damaged and destroyed.

Our children could see the anxious looks Tony and I had on our faces and knew instinctively of the importance of the broadcast. They started to ask questions.

"Mommy, will Japan come here and bomb our woods?" asked Beth. The boys laughed at her and Beth began to cry.

"All of you, be quiet. I need to hear this," threatened Tony. President Franklin Roosevelt announced he would speak to our nation the next day on December 8. We gathered to hear him.

"This is a history-making speech. We don't want to miss a word. Be quiet now until it's over," Tony announced while he turned up the volume. I will never forget the sound of the president's voice as it echoed through the house. He declared war against Japan. When done, the children joined us in conversation. The boys wanted to quit school and join the Navy.

"You're not old enough. I don't want to hear any more talk about quitting school," Tony said. Clare entertained Beth who quickly forgot the threatening atmosphere.

Everyone talked about the war. No matter who you saw or where you went, war became the topic of conversation. Little did we know how much the war would change our life.

～　　～　　～

Families were preparing for Christmas. Thousands of young men across our nation didn't wait for December 25 to volunteer. They enlisted into the services following the declaration of war. Young men across our nation, aged seventeen years old and up, were given a number and would be called to duty accordingly. This list, known as the "draft," became abolished in 1973 when our military forces became all volunteer.

The weather continued to be mild through December. In the middle of the month, a flu epidemic became widespread. Family after family were stricken. We were of no exception. Two days before the holiday, the children became ill. Tony and I followed. Mom and Dad did not join us for the holidays as planned. Both of them had the flu and felt it best to stay home.

We tried to enjoy Christmas but were too sick to do anything except lie in bed. Sometimes the children put their pillows on the floor, close to the decorated tree, covered themselves with blankets, and watched the train go 'round. I couldn't cook our Christmas dinner. None of us were able to eat normal meals. We did enjoy listening to holiday stories and traditional carols broadcast on the radio.

The first week of the new year found most everyone recovered. But my father had developed complications from his flu. He assured Mother she had nothing to worry about. Mom repeated his assurance but knew in her heart his illness had become serious. He had developed pneumonia. Fighting hard, he tried to overcome his congestion. Dad did not have a strong-enough immune system to fight off the virus. He passed in the middle of the night two weeks into January. As Mother had said, "A warm Christmas fills the cemetery."

All of us missed him. We worried about Mom being alone. She and Dad had been married for forty-eight years. She missed him terribly. My brother and sisters lived out of the area. After the funeral, they needed to go back to work and their homes. Mom found herself alone for the first time in her life. She had married Dad following her graduation from high school. Most young ladies of her day did not finish school. She met Dad in class, and they were sweethearts before graduation.

Tony called me into the living room a few weeks after the funeral. "Come on, Babe, sit with me. I have an idea I want to talk to you about," he said as he patted his hand where he wanted me to sit. Again, Tony knew what I needed before I did.

"I know you are worried about your Mother living alone. Why don't we ask her to move in with us? We could redecorate the first-floor bedroom into a nice room for your mom. You and I could take one of the upstairs bedrooms. I'll build two bedrooms downstairs for the boys. I think they would like to have their own rooms downstairs. A den of their own. What do you think of the idea?"

"Sounds like a great plan. I would like her here with us instead of being alone all the time. You're right, I am worried about her. How long do you think it would take to do all this?"

"I figure it would take about a month of weekends. The boys are big enough to be of help. If I know them, working on rooms for themselves, we might set some kind of construction record," Tony joked.

"I'll talk it over with Mom first thing tomorrow. I can't wait to ask her. I hope she likes the idea," I answered.

Tony talked to the boys about new bedrooms. Just as he thought, they were eager. When I talked to Mom about the move, she said, "Are you sure? I won't be any trouble or in the way?"

"Of course you're not any trouble. The children are excited about the thought of you living with us. Beth is excited because she thinks you might play dolls with her."

"It would be nice to be with family. Let's try it and see how it works out," Mom answered.

The bedrooms were completed and Mother's room was decorated. Mom and I were excited the day of the move. We were glad to have her with us. She could sense our love and appreciation for her and she appeared content.

After three months, Mom said one night after dinner, "What do you say, guys? I like it around here. I think I'm going to stay. You're stuck with me now. Let's sell my house." We were all happy with her decision.

"Now, Grandma, you can play dolls with me all the time," giggled Beth. We put her house on the market and it sold quickly.

I don't know if she knew how helpful she had become. When I was busy, she answered the phone. If Tony needed me at the station, I could go immediately. Sometimes she started dinner or baked one of her wonderful pies. Having her around was truly a blessing—a gift to the whole family.

CHAPTER 14

War Then Peace

Life as we knew it changed almost instantly with the attack on Pearl Harbor. Deeply involved in World War II, the USA fought with their allies on two fronts to stop Nazi Germany and halt Japan's attacks in the Philippines.

Americans focused their thoughts on one idea: to beat their enemies. They supported the war nonstop, with determination to foster peace and bring every soldier home. Patriotism skyrocketed to all-time highs.

Rations became an everyday word. Eggs, butter, meat, gasoline, silk hosiery, and even bread were distributed by coupon. The list ran on and on. Black market items greased the pockets of thieves. Could the America of today envision the ration of shoes? One pair a year per household member.

Clare walked back and forth to school every day and waitressed part-time. She wore out her leathered sole shoes rapidly.

"Mom, the hole in the bottom of my shoe is as big as a dime. Dirt stains my socks. I need new shoes!"

"We could pick up a black-market shoe coupon but the price is too high. Put a heavy piece of cardboard over the hole inside the shoe. We should get our yearly shoe coupons soon."

"If it rains, I'll wear my boots," Clare said.

A large part of our nation's workforce became women. No longer in the role of housewives, they worked on factory assembly lines.

Most industry of the day changed over to make machinery for use on war fronts. Rationed gasoline made for extra bookwork for Tony and Jim. Gas sales dropped. Our repair services carried us financially. Incomes, though reduced, remained stable.

During this time, Vera and Jim's family got to know Mother well. Calling her "Gran" became their norm. They assisted us in her move to our house. Mother's dining and front room furniture replaced our worn, outdated pieces.

"Beautiful!" Vera teased. "Now you're a Miss Fancy Pants."

"You think so? Yours is pretty darn nice too!"

One Sunday afternoon when they joined us for Sunday dinner, we discussed what we could do in Granite for the war effort. Mom's suggestion was met with favor. "Nearby towns have memorials to honor their servicemen. Granite doesn't. Why don't we have one?"

"I guess no one thought of it," I said. "At least ten boys from Granite are in the service. We should have done this long ago. Let's go to the next town meeting and suggest it when they ask for new business."

We attended the meeting and Jim brought the memorial idea to the floor. Our towns' people agreed. Mr. Powdy from the general hardware store offered to get the lowest prices possible on materials. A special committee composed of our town's most talented artists and construction workers met to design Granite's memorial. Plans included a large, curved, dark-speckled granite wall centered on the lawn where the crossroads met alongside our community park.

Metal plates with the names of Granite servicemen on one end and individual bronze plates with names of those killed in action on the opposite end. In the center was a flagpole with an American flag and flood lights. Around the wall, a cement-encircled sidewalk with a resting bench at each end faced the nameplates.

After the plans were approved, donations covered the costs. Granite's Women's Auxiliary Club participated in fundraising. As members, Vera, Mom, and I helped with bake sales and benefit chicken dinners. Selling refreshments at the Granite snowshoe baseball game proved entertaining for all, including the workers.

"Get your soda here! Ice-cold soda! Twenty-five cent ice-cold soda! Get your soda here!" bellowed Mom.

"Hot dogs! Hot dogs here! Get your hot dogs here!" I yelled. We stole glances of each other, and we laughed. We deliberately tried to outyell each other.

~   ~   ~

Unable to work in factories like women in bigger cities, we supported the war effort in our own small-town way. We raised money and covered all costs for the monument within a year. Ground broke the following spring, followed by the first town's Decoration Day service; the holiday is called Memorial Day now.

By 1945, the war had swung in our favor. Joy! Joy, but a short-lived joy. On April 12, 1945, our beloved President Franklin Roosevelt died suddenly. Our leader for twelve years, his federal programs and reforms had put our nation back on its feet during the Depression. Many felt that he was indispensable. He guided us through most of World War II. I knew of no one who didn't love him. Citizens cried in public, "Our Teddy died."

The school principal allowed teachers to play radios in the classrooms the day of Roosevelt's funeral. Children and adults sat in silence. Students and teachers wept alike. Vice President Harry Truman became president. After Berlin fell, the Germans withdrew. Truman concluded the war with Japan by ordering the drop of the first atomic bomb on Hiroshima. Even then, Japan refused to end the war. A second bomb forced surrender on August 14, 1945. On August 15, 1945, America celebrated victory over Japan, known to all as VJ Day. Church bells rang, music sounded. Citizens danced in the streets. Our church held a special service to give thanks. Americans from all walks of life celebrated the wars' end.

By the grace of God, our boys had not been drafted. Our servicemen gradually returned home. Families reunited. Peace prevailed.

CHAPTER 15

Destiny

As I picked up the phone, I could hear a voice ranting before I got it to my ear. It sounded like Jim. "Hello."

"Babe, David got burned. You and Tony have to get here right away."

"What happened?"

"A customer asked Dave to open their overheated radiator. He did and it exploded hot water and steam all over his face, chest, and arms. He's burnt bad."

"Oh my god! David took the car."

"I'm on my way," said Jim.

I ran to the family who were painting the house. "David got burned by a car radiator. It exploded. We've got to get there as fast as possible. Jim's coming to get us."

Shocked, Tony didn't say a word, dropped his paint brush, and scrambled out to the driveway with me to meet Jim. "He's got to be okay. He took my place today so I could stay home and paint the house," Tony said. Jim arrived within minutes and raced us back to the station. Dust flew. We found David on the floor propped against a two-tire sales display. The black rubber on the tires alongside his face made his skin look like a broiled red lobster. His eyes met ours. Tears ran down his burnt cheeks. "It hurts," he whispered as he barely spoke.

Tony paced and yelled, "Where's that ——? Did you recognize him?"

64

"Nope, never saw him before. He asked Dave to open the cap," Jim said.

"He knew it was hot. He let my kid open it. I'll kill that ——."

"Take it easy, Tony. He's gone. Left as soon as it happened."

I knelt close to David as he moaned. He was in shock. "It hurts, Mom, it hurts."

"Okay, honey. We'll get you to the hospital," I promised.

"I swear, If I ever get my hands on him—" Tony said.

"Come on, Tony, it's done. The guy's gone. Help Babe take Dave to the hospital," Jim said.

"Yeah! But if I ever meet the guy, I'll beat the —— out of him. The —— knew the water was hot. He wanted it opened, so he let my boy do it!" His temperament changed when he shifted his attention to David.

"I'll be as gentle as possible. I know it hurts," Tony said as he lifted and carried his son to the car. David groaned with every move.

"Watch him while I drive, Babe."

Tony had quieted. Slow to fester, this was a side of Tony I had never seen. Where did his treacherous anger come from? Were all Dads like this? When it comes to family, he'd fight the world, but this angry Tony is a man I didn't know. Heartsick, he hadn't been there to protect his son. He could never accept anyone hurting his family. I never knew swear words were in his vocabulary.

A freight train with at least a hundred cars blocked our way. An engine pulled while another on the back pushed. My stomach hurt. Tears filled my eyes. "Oh, Lord, please help us to get David to the hospital safely," I begged. I never felt more helpless. Why this train delay?

David lost consciousness. Tony's fingers tapped the steering wheel nonstop. His eyes popped, glued on every passing train car.

A medical team met us at the emergency room door as Jim had called the hospital ahead. Pain control being our first concern, we felt relieved when the hospital team treated him accordingly.

In the Northwoods, we hadn't expected a foreign doctor. His bushy black hair and mustache went well with his broken English. "Your boy has first- and second-degree burns over his face, arms, and chest. He needs to be admitted."

"How will you treat him? Will he scar?" I asked.

"Infection is a concern. His face has first-degree damage while parts of his chest and arms have second. Without complications, he should be fine and back home in a few days. Sulfa drugs to prevent infection and pain meds will treat his discomfort. Someone should stay with him. The pain makes him agitated."

"Of course one of us will be with him," Tony said.

"I'll stay first," I offered. "It's ten o'clock. You go home and sleep a while. We can take turns," I answered.

"Are you sure you are all right? I'll come early tomorrow to relieve you. Dave is going to be all right, I'm sure of it. After all, he's a chip off the old block, right?" Tony winked.

"You always could make me smile. Yes, I'll be fine."

Tony told Mom and Jim about David needing bedside care. Vera, Jim, and Mother all helped. Everyone pitched in. Business, home, and hospital ran smoothly during David's confinement. On the way home from being discharged, David said, "I'll never open a hot radiator cap again ever. I'll never touch another one. My face is peeling. It's scary, but I'm glad I'm not going to scar."

"Take your time to heal, son. Get back on your feet before you try to work at the station," Tony said.

"Dad, we need to talk. I know you want to keep the station in the family, but I don't want to work there anymore. I'm graduating next spring. I want to be a journalist. I'll work for you until I leave high school because I'll need a full-time summer job to earn money for college. I can't help it. I'm not mechanical." Tony knew David should pursue his dream just as Tony had when he studied art and moved to the Northwoods. He understood.

"Sure, Dave. I get it," he said with hidden disappointment. "A man's gotta do what he's gotta do. I'll put you on a full-time schedule for the summer."

Hearing this, I recalled how young Tony and I were when we met. He was a college student close to David's age. Now it was my little boy's turn to grow up and face life's challenges and destiny.

CHAPTER 16

Painting Apples

I sat staring out the kitchen window. My eyes filled with tears. Tightness in my chest mimicked a heart attack and my stomach painfully hurt. My mind told me it's okay. Time is passing; I wanted it to stop. The older the children became, the faster it passed. I didn't want them to ever grow up. Day after day melted away, like butter heated over low heat. I couldn't stop it. This is our life.

David had graduated from high school and established a new routine in college. One already grown and ready to take on the world. Clare turned sixteen. A pretty young lady, built small with long reddish-brown hair, always pulled back into a ponytail, it swayed when she walked. Her eyes were light brown and accompanied a gentle disposition. She would step aside to keep from walking on an ant. Although Tony would never admit it, Clare was his "Little Sweetie" and would always be.

Shortly after Clare's sixteenth birthday, she went on her first date with a boy from school. They went to a football game. Tony frowned for a week. Under his breath, he would make comments he thought no one heard. "She's too young. She doesn't need to go on dates. She can go to football games with her brothers." Mumble mumble.

"You know, Tony, Clare has to grow up too. Time marches on," I said. As time passed, eventually Tony became more comfortable with Clare's social life, but his rules for dating were still somewhat strict compared to today's standards.

"Your dates have to come in the house to pick you up. Mother and I need to know who they are and you need to be home by 11:00 p.m."

"Okay, Dad, we're good," Clare would answer. Tony often announced expectations. Our daughter always nodded her head "yes" and never rebelled. She didn't seem to resent his authority.

Clare met a young man named Rodger who traveled back and forth from school with David. Being handsome, blond, blue-eyed, and artistic, he reminded me of a young Tony. Working for a degree in art, he wanted to teach. He and David shared the same dorm and town. They took turns driving home on weekends. Rodger and Clare dated for a year.

One afternoon Clare sat on the front porch and asked me to join her. "Mom, I have to tell you that Rodger and I want to get married. I love him so much. I don't know how to tell Dad." I had sensed their affection for each other and could feel passion in her voice.

Although Rodger is artistic like Tony, he is a different type of man. Rodger's sense of humor led the way in all of his relationships. People were comfortable and loved being around him. He liked to laugh and party and favored modern art. Would Tony understand these differences?

"I wouldn't worry that Dad will disapprove. Sometimes his bark is worse than his bite. Would you like me to be with you when you tell him?"

"That would really help. I am unsure of what to say. I don't know if I should blurt it out or kind of work around the idea first."

"I think you'll find the words naturally. You and Dad have always been close. He just wants things to be good for you. Talk with him like you are with me."

After we paused for a few minutes, Clare said, "You're right, Mom, it will work out. Come with me anyway, okay?"

After dinner, we cornered Tony when he sat in his easy chair to listen to the radio. Clare looked into Tony's eyes and said, "Daddy, I want to marry Rodger."

"You what? You want to get married? You can't marry him. He doesn't know how to work. He's just a kid. He can't earn a living by 'painting apples.' He might like art but it won't put food on the table."

With tears in her eyes, Clare answered, "Daddy, I love him so much. We can make it. I know we can."

"You're both just kids. Come back to me when you're older and have a man who knows how to work." Tony didn't approve! Clare wept hysterically. She went out on the porch where she cried on brother Bob's shoulder.

"Come on, Tony! She's not a baby anymore and she really loves Rodger. Remember when we were young? How we felt? We only had the cabin to start with. Look at us today. Rodger will have his degree in another year and a half. He'll be able to teach. They'll make out all right. If they still feel the same way when he graduates, we need to say yes. If we don't, Clare will be crushed. You don't want to do this, do you?"

"I suppose you're right. You usually are. I'll tell her we will talk about marriage if they still feel the same when he graduates." Tony went out on the porch and sat by Clare.

"Okay, honey. If you still feel the same after Rodger finishes school, we'll talk about marriage." Relieved, Clare hugged her Dad and smiled while her feet began to dance up and down like the cha-cha-cha. The look on Tony's face overran with outside smiles and inward sadness. He slowly let loose of the little girl who had always clung to him. In his eyes, she began to look like the young woman she had become.

The two young lovers continued to date. Their admiration for each other showed in their idolizing stares. Rodger visited our home more often. We began to know and appreciate him. Tony had a hard time staying composed when Rodger giggled. It seemed immature. Clare loved the sound. She continued to adore her man.

Tony and I noticed Rodger didn't manage money very well. I asked Clare about it. "Rodger doesn't seem to know how to handle his debts. Are you okay with this?"

"I don't care because I know how. I'll teach him after we get married. Mom, I'm not concerned."

"You can't change someone because you're a couple. Everyone has a fault or two or they wouldn't be human. Are you ready to overlook his faults? If you're not, now's not the time to marry."

Clare loved her sweetheart as is. She admired his good traits and there were many. They were happy together.

When Rodger started his last semester in school, discussing the wedding wasn't necessary. The plans had become accepted by all of us. Tony had surrendered to the idea his future son-in-law would support his daughter by "painting apples."

CHAPTER 17

Creepy Crawlers

Invaded by millions of creepy green-and-white-striped worms a few short weeks before Clare's wedding became an unexpected nightmare. Driving us all to our wits' end, we fought them every waking moment. They covered everything in sight. The battle never ceased and it started in the spring when David and Rodger graduated from college.

After graduation, Dave found work writing for a Chicago newspaper. Our family celebrated his success as though the bewitching twelve o'clock hour had been reached on New Year's Eve. His job demanded presence one week after graduation. Abruptly, he moved to Illinois. Goodbye hugs and tears followed him out to his well-packed car as he left.

Rodger found an art teacher position in a grade school eighty miles from Granite. His job would not begin until September classes resumed. He needed work to carry over. While in high school, he worked at Mr. Powdy's general hardware store during the summer. Mr. Powdy rehired him. Rodger liked working in town, keeping him close to his bride-to-be.

Clare and Rodger talked with Pastor Bill about their wedding plans. "The community center has a Saturday not reserved in the middle of June. We would like to book it for our reception if we can coordinate the ceremony here at the church on the same day," Rodger said.

"Saturday the eighteenth is available. I can marry you in the early afternoon if the time will work for you," Pastor answered.

"Three o'clock would be better. A buffet supper could follow in this time frame. Is it possible?" Clare asked.

"I can make some changes in my schedule. We can plan on three." Reservations for the eighteenth of June became a reality.

Mr. Powdy's general and hardware store had been Granite's only general shopping source for the past thirty years. Merchandise needed and not displayed could be ordered through catalogs. Town residents routinely purchased orders through the store. We were no exception.

As a little girl, Clare liked to look at clothes in Mr. Powdy's catalogs. When she looked at the bridal gowns, she'd say, "Someday, Mom, I am going to get married in one of these pretty dresses." She didn't forget Grandma had offered to make her gown, but her heart led her to get the gown in the bridal book.

"I found one I like. It's very simple with three-quarter-length sleeves embroidered in satin. The neckline has the same design. As the full skirt swings, you can see the short train. I love it! Fifty dollars is a lot but I have extra money from tips. I know you'll love it, Mother."

"Dad and I will buy it. This is a fair price for a nicely made garment. On your day off, why don't we go to the store and look at all the bridal clothes? Grandma, Beth, and I need outfits too. Could your bridesmaid, Cathy, join us? Maybe she would like to pick out something with you there."

We chose to go the next Wednesday. Excited, we got up at the crack of dawn to be ready early. Cathy joined us. Tony drove the five of us to the store in time for its opening. Mr. Powdy greeted us. His smile reached ear to ear as he said, "Never thought I would see the day little Clare and Rodger would look at their marriage outfits in my store. You grew up so darn fast. I'll keep Rodger busy up front and you ladies can sit at the back table. Take your time. There are some tea bags and a tea kettle on the stove back there. You can find the cups in the cabinet. Have some tea while you look things over. Take as long as you like."

Rodger came back to say hello and get a hug from Clare. As he left, he laughed and said, "Don't worry, I'll stay away."

Again, I could see the resemblance of Rodger to a young Tony as Rodger's blond hair fell in his eyes as he turned. Uncanny!

We spent three hours in the shop. Clare picked a soft pastel pink for her bridesmaids' outfit. Both girls liked it. Clare had described her gown well: fashionable yet simple. Gran wanted to make her veil. We picked out an iridescent pearl-flowered crown to attach it to. Perfect! Mom ordered the materials. We finished making choices after we picked out white shoes for all of the ladies. After all, it is close to Decoration Day when the wearing of summer-weight begins.

The men in the nuptial party decided to wear dress suits with white shirts, blue ties, and mirror-polished black shoes. What a handsome group they would be.

"I know how to make artificial flowers. I would like to make them for our ceremony. It would save us a lot of money. What do you think? You could help me, and we could finish in time," Rodger said.

"Make some for me first. I would like to see them before I decide," Clare answered.

"Okay, I'll make some tonight. I'd like to make a wedding-style generic poster to invite everyone in town. I could post it on the town board. We won't have to send out individual invitations. This will save us a lot of money. What do you think?"

"I am amazed you are so fugal. Didn't know you had it in you. Of course I'll help you. I like both ideas," Clare answered. Rodger's ideas were workable. Together, the bride and groom took care of the flowers and invitations.

When Decoration Day came on May 30, a traditional community picnic took place in the town park after hanging a wreath on the memorial wall.

"Babe, you better decide on the menu for the wedding supper. We're two weeks away from the day."

"What do you have in mind?" asked Grandma.

"You're right, we should. Now, while most everyone in town is at the park, let's talk about it."

Most of the women sat at picnic tables circled around the bar-
becue grill. We joined them in visiting one another. The men gathered for horseshoes across the road. We cheered them on in between
conversations.

Vera shirked, "Ewww! What are all those green caterpillars piled
up on the grass?"

"Oh, they're nothing to worry about. I see bunches of them off
and on every spring. They don't bite anyone. They're just around," I
said as I started the conversation about the menu.

"For the reception meal, Tony and I have decided on roasted
chicken cooked on a spit. Jim and Tony built a large one. It holds
twenty chickens. Bobby and his friends offered to turn it."

"Let's hope the weather is nice so you can cook outside. I'd like
to make the baked beans and biscuits," volunteered Mom. The other
women cross-fired with "potluck" ideas for side dishes and relish
trays. Mr. Powdy offered the use of a juke box he had stored in his
garage. Rodger and Clare liked the idea. Now they could have dance
music without expense.

There are advantages to living in a small town. Everyone knows
one another. When occasions rise with need for "family style dedica-
tion," it's there. Clare and Rodger grew up with these neighbors who
loved them and wanted to be a part of their celebration.

While we made plans, Beth came screaming into the circle.
"Mommy, there are snakes everywhere."

"No, honey. They're caterpillars. They won't hurt you."

With tears running down her cheeks, Beth said, "There's so
many, Mommy."

Tony picked frightened Beth up and placed her on a picnic
table. We all took note of Beth's discovery and laughed as we thought
nothing of the hefty number.

At dusk when the mosquitoes made their appearance, we needed
to leave. Singing "Good Night Sweetheart" and laughing, we waved
goodbye to our friends as we carried our picnic gear back to the car.
When we arrived home, we noticed that clumps of the wormlike
creatures had crawled onto our porch.

"There are sure a lot of them this year," I said while I hopped from spot to spot to avoid them. Tony carried Beth into the house because she shivered with fear.

The next day we opened our front door to fetch a newspaper and found our veranda, most of the outside walls, and pathway to the garage covered with thousands of little green-and-white-striped worms. "I never saw a hatch this big. Give me the broom!" yelled Tony. Sweeping as fast as he could, he tried to brush them away. As fast as he pushed them aside, others appeared. The battle was lost.

"Stay in the house. Keep the doors and windows shut. I'll go to the station and see how widespread this is," Tony yelled.

He soon returned.

"The hatch is enormous. Everything's covered. The old-timers say they have never seen so many before. The Forest Rangers told us you could wash them off with soapy water and pressure from a hose. They're called tent caterpillars. They eat tree foliage. When the trees are close enough to each other, the caterpillars form webs from one tree to another. If you're in a woodsy area and stand still to listen, you can hear them by the thousands eating the leaves," Tony said.

"We should turn on the radio. Maybe there will be news about the invasion," I said. We listened to reports the rest of the day. Frequent news briefs about the creatures interrupted programs. Interviews with local Rangers were often. The Rangers knew the most about them. One suggested coating the bottom of trees with Vaseline and where the lubrication stops, furnace tape should be wrapped around the trunks. These barriers would keep most of them from climbing up. Reports stated they would be abundant from the end of May until the end of June. During this time, they spin their cocoons, hibernate, and emerge as moths.

"Those pests will still be around when it's time for the wedding. I can't imagine Clare's long skirt brushing across those nasty things," I said.

"I think a lot of them will be in a cocoon state by then. Not all of them, but some. I'll make sure someone sweeps the path for Clare, from the car to inside the church. I hope they're still not all over the place by then." Tony sighed.

Every day, Tony and I hosed our buildings down. It didn't take long for dead carcasses to pile up. They smelled horrible, like old, rotten cheese. Now we had to fight the stench as well as the critters. Anthony, Bob, and I wheel barreled dead ones away. Taking them far away from the house to dump helped to dissipate the stinky odor. When I slept, parades of tent larvae floated through my mind. I had seen so many I couldn't forget them.

The children and I kept things under control at the house. Tony fought them at the station. While we fought the ugly things, we learned Clare's dress order could not be filled. It had been put on back order. Being upset, Clare cried most of the day. "It's too late now to find another dress. What will I do?" she wept.

Vera offered her wedding gown. "I think the dress is about Clare's size. You're welcome to use it if you think it will do. It can be 'something barrowed.'"

Clare tried it on and much to her surprise, it fit like a glove. Styled close to what she had picked, her face lit up like a Christmas tree. She realized she would be able to get married in a gorgeous gown after all. Clare hugged Vera and said, "Thank you so much. Gran finished my veil and it matches the dress perfectly."

Grandma gently pressed every wrinkle out of the gown and displayed it in Clare's room. It looked beautiful and new. During the following week, the rest of the pressing got done. The clothes, shoes, flowers, cake, and "Just Married" car sign managed completion on time. We needed to get the juke box to the community center two blocks away. The boys and Clare decided they would push it. The box had rollers on each corner.

"Don't worry, Mom. Anthony, Clare, and I will do it. It will roll easy," said Bobby.

"Don't forget to wear your boots. You'll stomp on a lot of those crawly things walking down the street. I'll meet you at the center later." They left before I finished my coffee.

Mr. Powdy went along with their plan. "After you get it in the center, plug it in and test it. Make sure it works," he suggested. They pushed and pulled over the pests, making crunchy-like sounds.

When they arrived, the critters covered the entrance door, making Clare angry.

"I'm going to have dance music! No matter what!" She took off her boot and used it to beat and smash them then swiped the pests away. The music maker played well when cleaned up and plugged in. The children decided to steal a few minutes for fun and took time to dance. I could hear them laughing while I hung decorations on the other side of the room. I called them to help me place tables and chairs across the massive gym floor. The space doubled for sports and community events.

The wedding day arrived. All had been accomplished. The weather turned cloudy and cool which caused the critters to be less active. Perfect! Everyone arrived at the church on time. Mom played the organ for Clare's entrance. She looked beautiful when she smiled while holding Tony's arm. Together, they slowly stepped forward down the aisle. Rodger stood tall while he waited for his bride. When Tony presented his once "little sweetie" to the arms of the man she loved, I detected a tear. I already had tears on my cheeks. Clare became Mrs. Rodger Brent.

When Tony came to sit in our pew, he reached for my hand and affectionately squeezed. Without words, we felt each other's pride created by our lovely daughter.

"Creepy Crawlers" didn't keep us from enjoying one of the most precious days of our lives.

CHAPTER 18

Betrayal

Yumpa! Yumpa! Yumpa! The catchy beat of polkas could be heard a block away. Laughter, singing, the stomp of feet vibrated the walls of the community center. Granite never had a grander wedding celebration. Clare and Rodger had chosen the perfect place for their reception.

Our buffet supper had followed the church ceremony with an open bar provided by Rodger's family. After the bride and groom danced their traditional first dance, the juke box pulsated every beat of nonstop music. Everyone joined them, including the children. Jim, Vera, Tony, and I tripped the light fantastic. If we weren't stomping, we jitterbugged. Sweated up and out of breath, we took a break and sat at one of the side tables. We quenched our thirst with cold drinks.

"I'm going outside with the boys to decorate Rodger's car. They'll be leaving for their honeymoon after the wedding cake is served. Those cans have to rattle all the way to wherever they're going," Tony said.

"Good idea. Have you got all you need?" I asked.

"Yep, put it together ahead of time."

Clare and Rodger cut the first piece of cake and served it to each other. Crumbs and frosting decorated their faces. Smiling guests clapped. Vera, Mom, and I served 120 servings of cake. The bride and groom left. Tony and I watched them drive away with a "Just Married" sign, streamers rippling out of the side windows, and a half dozen tin cans hanging from their back bumper. We could hear them rattle a song when they bounced to and fro on the pavement.

"Nice job, hon. The car looks very newly married," I jested.

Some of the guests departed after Clare and Rodger left. Remaining neighbors continued to dance. Music from the juke kept their feet tapping.

At nine thirty, Tony took Mom and Beth home. When he returned, we danced and visited with neighbors. By eleven, everyone had left. Vera offered to help clean up glasses on the tables and take some of the refrigerated leftovers to our car. Tony gathered trash. Carefully, we carried our cargo across the parking lot. As we trotted along, we could see a couple passionately embraced. We turned our heads aside to avoid staring. We giggled.

On the way back, we almost bumped into them. They had moved. No longer embracing, we could see their faces. Our foreheads frowned and our mouths dropped open as we glared at the couple we saw. Could we really be seeing this? Oh my god! It was Jim and a young woman, perhaps in her twenties.

I lifted my hand to cover my mouth to keep from yelling. Vera froze as she stared at Jim. Suddenly she turned and ran toward the center. I followed.

When I caught up, she had sat down at a table with her head buried in her arms while she tried to muffle the sounds of crying screams. How do you comfort your best friend's pain? I put my arms around her and whispered, "Vera, I'm so sorry."

Tony saw us and came over immediately. "What's going on? Where's Jim?" I pulled him to the side and quietly told him what happened. Vera lifted her head and tear-stained face and asked, "Tony, will you take me home?"

As Tony started to answer, Jim came stumbling up to their table. "You aren't taking her anywhere. She's my wife. I'll take her home," he angrily said with slurred speech.

"Okay, but come with me first to get a cup of coffee. Lean on me," Tony said. After a few shoves from Jim, Tony escorted him to a table on the other side of the room. With coaxing, Jim agreed to drink a cup of coffee. Once he quieted down, he allowed Tony to drive.

Approaching us with Jim at his side, Tony said, "I'll take both of you home. Vera can sit in the back with you, Babe. I'll sit Jim up front with me." It took both Tony and I to get Jim into the front seat. We took them home and Tony put his staggering friend to bed.

I hugged Vera and told her to call if she needed help. Tony and I returned to the center to finish the cleanup. I kept shaking my head in disbelief. "How could Jim do such an awful thing to Vera? He's betrayed her. I wonder if things will ever be the same?" I said.

"The drinking is what caused him to act like this. I wonder how much he had?"

"I don't know what we can do to help. We can't judge them or tell them what to do, but we could pray for them," I said.

"Right now, that is all we can do. They need to work things out themselves."

CHAPTER 19

Chapters

"It's downright disgraceful what's happened to them. I want to punch Jim right in his face. I miss Vera and the kids so much. What exactly are we supposed to do? It's been two weeks since I've seen them," I complained.

"I don't know what to do anymore either. I see Jim every day at work. I never said anything about it before, but Jim has been coming in with liquor on his breath off and on for the past six months. I'm starting to believe there is a problem. He's hidden it well," Tony answered.

We decided to go about our daily routines and stay out of their problems. We stopped all activities the four of us had done together. It became a challenge to keep out of their personal life yet be available if needed.

Because of our friendship, both Tony and I felt a gnawing sense of loss. Keeping a reasonable distance, we prayed they would resolve their dilemma. "There is nothing we can do but pray the Lord will help them make the right decisions," Tony said.

"He will. I hope they remember how much the Lord loves them and wants the best for them. Let's keep on praying."

Vera called. "Is it all right if I come over for a while? I need to talk with you. You're the only person I can trust who won't repeat our conversation to anyone. The kids are in school. It would be a good time to come."

"Sure, the back door's open."

When she came in, I could see the serious unemotional stare on her face. When she became seated at the table, I said, "How about a cup of coffee? Do you still use cream?"

We kept our cups full as we talked two hours away. "I can't make up my mind if I should leave Jim or not," concluded Vera with an angry look in her eyes.

"I hoped you two could make up."

"I don't think I want to. Jim still drinks every day and he is so darn mean. He hates the world and wants to get his own station in Rice Lake, sell the house, and move there."

"It's not for me to say what you should do. You're the only one whose heart knows the answer. We feel bad about what's going on. Is there any way we can help?"

With tears now running down her cheeks, she answered, "You can't. I don't come around much because I am embarrassed about this whole mess. The children are upset. They can sense what isn't spoken. I don't know what to do," Vera cried.

I put my arm around her and said, "I know you well enough to know you will do what is right for you and the children, whatever it might be. I'm so sorry."

"The kids will be home soon. I need to go. I don't know when I will see you again."

"Anytime, Vera, whatever works for you."

Tony came home with the boys, on schedule. After dinner, he asked the children to clean up from supper and do the dishes. He invited me to come into the living room and sit beside him. "I want to talk to you about the station. Jim told me today he wants to dissolve our partnership. There's a new pumper going in at Rice Lake. He wants to buy it and have his own place. The only fair way for us to split it is to establish the business' worth and each take half. I figure it's value to be $80,000.00. We should each get $40,000.00. What do you think?"

"Well, sure. It's the only fair thing to do. Did he mention Vera? She came over today. They have not made up and Jim is still drinking."

"I can smell it on him. I just didn't mention it much because I hoped he would stop. We have been friends for so long. It's hard. I guess a split could be a good thing. He shouldn't be around the station with liquor on his breath. It's dangerous around machinery and the customers don't want a drinking mechanic to work on their car. Maybe he'll straighten out if he has full responsibility of a business. I can raise the money to keep the station. I'll buy him out."

"I'm glad you still want the station. Let's give it all we've got. Go ahead."

Tony took care of the paperwork, which dissolved the partnership. We bought out Jim's half and now had sole ownership.

With Jim and his boys gone, we became shorthanded. Tony hired a mechanic who had a business of his own at one time and didn't need a lot of training. Twenty-five-year-old Charlie worked part-time at the pumps until the boys came in after school. I didn't hear from Vera very often. I called her from time to time to let her know I cared. The sparkle in her voice had vanished and the Vera I knew and loved seemed to be gone.

She called me one day and said, "We sold the house and plan to move to Rice Lake. Would you and Tony help us load the moving truck? I'm leaving some things here for the new owners, so there isn't much to be moved."

"Okay, we'll help you."

Together, we loaded the truck. I missed the jokes we used to throw back and forth to one another. The definite quiet became eerie. When finished, a few nonemotional goodbyes took place, and nobody smiled or made any unnecessary eye contact. They drove the truck away.

The departure seemed so final that their leaving made all of us sad. We watched the two best friends we had pull away. The loss felt painful. Our children had grown up together. When they said goodbye to one another, tears flowed with their hugs to one another. Unsettled feelings prevailed.

One evening, when the sun became low in the Western sky, Tony and I went out to fish for walleye. They bite best at dusk. Calm waters reflected a vivid sunset, making a sight only our Creator could have planned. Slowly, Tony rowed along the shoreline as our lines dragged. *Biff! Bam! Wham!* We caught one night's supper after another. When the sun set, we already had more of a catch than we wished for.

"Babe, it is a shame Vera and Jim are gone. We spent so much time down by the lake together. Life can be like a book with many chapters. They became more than one chapter in our lives. We'll just have to close this one and start another. Sometimes I wonder what's around the corner."

"I know! It's us! Just us! You and me and nobody else, like when we first got married. I'm going to love it."

CHAPTER 20

Worthy Angel

I blamed myself. It's my fault. If I hadn't left Mom with a big wash, she wouldn't have gotten hurt. If only I hadn't been comfortable with her helping so much. I should have been there. I wish I could go back and change things. My heart aches because of what happened to her.

We had a hot summer. Being used to cool Canadian breezes, we sweated until our clothes were drenched. Finding relief perched on boat docks with our feet submerged in the cool water was the only comfort we found. How do people from the south survive in the heat?

Tony and the boys spent most of their time at the station and on slow days came home early to take a swim in the cool lake water. Of course, Mom and I washed more clothes than usual. The boys wore several changes daily. The humidity seemed unbearable. Saturated laundry filled our hampers to overflow.

On laundry days, Mom and I had worked as a team to finish before noon. One wash day, I left her alone because of an unexpected call for bookwork at the station.

"Go ahead, I'll start the laundry. You can help me when you get back," Mom said.

"Okay, I won't be long."

Tony brought me back in two hours. When I opened the front door, I yelled, "Mom, I'm home." I went to the basement, called again, "Mother, where are you?" Why doesn't she answer? No sound from the washer.

At the bottom of the stairs, I found Mom sprawled on the floor. She held her arm and laid in a peculiar position. Her eyes were closed.

"Mom, what happened?"

"I caught my arm," she bravely whispered. Her deformed black-and-blue arm had been caught up in the wringer of the washing machine. The washer shut off automatically as the rollers dislodged. When she yanked her arm free, her feet went out from underneath her. She fell and broke her right leg. Being in severe pain, Mother found it difficult to speak.

"Don't move. I'll get a pillow and call Dr. Arnold." I placed a supportive cushion under her head and called Tony too. They both arrived about the same time.

"You sure have a couple of nasty breaks. You're going to need a cast on your arm and leg. I can work here if you don't want to go to the hospital, but we'll have to move you upstairs. I can put splints on to move you. I have some ether in my bag. It can temporarily help with the pain. Expect to hurt a lot when we relocate you," Dr. Arnold said.

"I want to stay home. Take me upstairs," Mom tearfully answered.

The doctor applied the temporary supports and administered a mild sedative. We used an old kitchen door as a stretcher to carry Mother upstairs. Tony carried the top and Doc and I held bottom corners. Once transferred to her bed, she seemed more comfortable.

"There is too much swelling to cast today. We will have to wait until the swelling subsides. If I do it now, the plaster will become loose. Take aspirin every four hours for pain, stay in bed, and call me when the puffy areas subside. I'll come back. Put a pillow under her arm. This will help the pain and elevate it," Dr. Arnold requested.

"Okay, we will. Thank you for coming so quickly. I'll call when she is ready."

Mom had a lot of discomfort. She lay quiet with her eyes closed and complained little. I knew under the circumstances she missed my father more than ever. Mom's so brave. My special patient refused to eat and drink. When the doctor called, I told her of my concern. She instructed me to try and get Mom to drink more liquids. I encouraged her repeatedly without success.

My heart ached as I watched Mother grow weaker each day. It seemed as though she shut down and didn't care anymore. The casts were put on her arm and leg as planned. Eventually most of the pain decreased. It would be at least six to eight weeks before the plaster support could be removed.

She grew pale. Her sparkle was gone. She slept most of the time.

Beth became a big help in caring for Mother. She answered Mom's calls and played on the floor close to her bed. Tony visited frequently and told jokes to cheer her up. "Knock, knock," he would say.

"Who's there?"

"Olive."

"Olive who?"

"Olive you," he'd say with a silly grin.

We both watched Mother fail. I worried if she might not recover. "Do you see what I see? She looks so peaked and frail? Let's ask Pastor to stop and see her. This might lift her spirits," I said.

"It might help. She misses going to church. Do you want me to stop by and ask him?"

"Why don't you?"

Pastor Johnson came every few days. He kept us spiritually strong and prayed with us. Early one day, about six weeks after the accident, I went into her room and found her not breathing. When I touched her, she felt cold. I shook as the shock ran through my body. I realized she had died in her sleep. Even though I had figured her time here would be short, I still wasn't prepared to find her dead.

Her relaxed face radiated peace. Mom had become one of God's worthiest angels. She had always offered to help and sincerely seemed to love everyone. I remember once calling her the "Fix It Lady."

Tony, being home, comforted me, notified family, and helped me make burial arrangements.

"In Eagle River, there is a new business called a funeral parlor. It is a family service for people to wake their loved ones in a beautiful place and not use their home. A large nicely decorated area is used for casket viewing. Rows of velvet-cushioned chairs are plentiful for guests who come to pay their respects. A special car comes to the house to transport the deceased to the parlor and final resting place. Off to one side, another room offers buffet-type snacks and coffee. We can afford to do this. Would you consider it? It will be so much easier for all of us. If we call them now, they will come right away," Tony said.

"It sounds like a good idea, but It would feel like I've deserted her by taking her to a strange place," I said with tears in my eyes.

"Oh no, honey, your mom would have liked this. She always wanted what seemed best for you. She knew how hard it is on families to hold wakes at home. She would have liked this gorgeous place."

"I hope you're right. I am going to trust your judgment. You call them for us, okay?"

The funeral director came to the house. He requested the clothes we wanted Mom to be waked and buried in. Tony took me out into the backyard while the director and his assistant took Mom's body on a gurney and placed her in a big black double-doored car and drove off. Tony had removed me from the scene, knowing this would be hard for me to watch.

Many tears were shed during the wake and burial. After the funeral, my four siblings left to go back to their jobs and homes. They reassured me I had made the right choice by using the funeral parlor.

"I was surprised to see Vera and Jim drive in from Rice Lake to attend the funeral. I'm glad they remembered Mother. Vera said Susie is getting married and wanted to come back to her Granite church for the wedding. She and Jim will be in town often and they plan to stop and visit. It's nice to see them again," I said.

"It surprised me to see them too. It was like they still lived next door and never left," Tony answered.

"I hope they do visit often."

~　　~　　~

As time passed, I slowly became used to Mom not being here. Until my time of acceptance, I said to myself every time I left the house, "Goodbye, worthy angel."

CHAPTER 21

Unforgettable Storm

So cute! How did this soft white fluffy stranger walk into our lives and steal our affection? We didn't know she would give us one of the biggest scares of our life when she disappeared with our daughter.

We put a new work team together at the service station. Our lead mechanic left, which dismantled our entire schedule. We hired Mike to be our new mechanic and shop manager. Well-experienced, he fit into our routines perfectly.

Tony kept Charlie, who was a young father who wanted a second part-time job. He willingly pumped gas from ten to three until the boys came in after school. Tony filled in as needed. Once again, our team worked as smooth as a new shaving blade.

The winter's cold and slippery, snow-packed roads paved the way for us to be busy twelve to fourteen hours a day. Constantly, the snow-plow and tow-truck struggled to keep up with calls on a backed-up service list.

"You and the boys need to stop long enough to eat," I repeatedly told them. Seldom did they listen. I solved the problem by bringing hot food from home and putting it close to their noses' reach. The smell of hot chili or soup hypnotized them enough to sit down at the table set up in the back where they gobbled their food.

One cold day, a car arrived at the office door. Left open, a little white puppy pushed itself inside. "Tony! Tony, come here! Look what I found!" I squealed. A shaking, dirty, smelly mutt stood before me. I picked her up and held her close.

"Where in the world did she come from? Looks like a wild one. Several dogs hang around the station every morning when I open. I usually chase them off with the broom. This one is kind of cute. Must have stayed around to keep warm. Should we feed her and give her fresh water?" Tony took his lunch sandwich and broke it into small pieces to lay on the floor. He used his soup bowl for water and set it alongside the scraps.

"Now, little lady, how about some lunch?" he said as he moved her close to her feast. Being anxious, she led us to believe she hadn't eaten in a while. This little creature gulped down her food and water lickety-split.

"What a cutie. I wonder what breed she is," I asked.

"My guess? Some kind of poodle. Look how curly her coat is," Tony said.

"Beth has wanted a dog for some time. She's twelve and is old enough for pet responsibility. Wouldn't it be nice to surprise her and bring home this sweet little pup?" I rattled on.

The boys joined us in the office to view the treasure. "She must belong to somebody. We could ask around and see if we could find the owner," Bobby said.

"How about a 'Found Lost Dog' sign on the town board? That might help," Tony suggested. All of us agreed to look for her master. If not found in a reasonable length of time, we would bring her home.

After two weeks of honest effort, we could not locate the owner. It had been a chore to keep her hidden from Beth, but the surprise presentation made it worth the game of hide-and-seek. Tony brought the little white ball of fur home hidden under his heavy coat. When he came in the door, he called out, "Beth! Come here and help me take off this big jacket, will you?"

"Hi, Daddy, I'll help you." Out popped the pouch. Beth's mouth fell open. "Oh! Daddy! A puppy! A puppy! What a cute puppy!"

"This little one needs a home and love. Would you like to have her for your pet?" Beth beamed. Her nurturing instincts took over as she took the little stranger and cuddled her.

"She's all yours, honey! Take care of her and give her a name. You are in charge of food, water, and walks on a leash three times a day. You'll need to shovel her messes and dump them in the woods. Can you do this?"

"Oh yes! Yes, I can! But I don't know what to name her."

"Give her a girly name like Susie or something," teased Robert.

"Lady Bug," Beth whispered.

During dinner, we insisted Lady Bug not be allowed at the table. Surprisingly, she laid quietly in the living room while we ate. After dinner, Beth gave her dog a bath and brought her into the front room. The five of us watched the silly little entertainer run back and forth to dry her coat. When she rolled around on the floor and rubbed her fur against the furniture, we all laughed at her drama.

"Where should I keep her food and water bowls?" asked Beth.

"Someplace out of the way of kitchen traffic," I answered.

The dog's food containers were placed. Lady Bug rushed over to them and slurped her dinner. After a hearty meal, the new family member fell asleep on Beth's lap. At bedtime, our daughter took her new pet into her bed. "It would be much better to give Lady Bug her own place to sleep. I have some older quilts I can give you for her bed. Would you like to use them?" I asked.

Gathered in Beth's room, we watched her make the covers into a meticulous pile. Lady Bug had no part of this neatness. She pawed from side to side and scratched and dug until she fluffed her new bed into a satisfactory heap. All of us laughed at her.

When Beth finally went to bed for the night, she said, "Mom, I think I'll call Lady Bug 'Lady.' She's not a bug."

"Good idea, honey. Lady, it will be."

All of us drifted off to sleep as we thought about our new family member. While we slept, the wind whistled, the temperature plummeted, and snow mounted. The Grinch of winter made a grand blizzard entrance. I rose early and started to cook breakfast. I could hear the boys move around upstairs. Beth would always come into the kitchen before the boys and help me set the table, but she didn't volunteer this morning.

The smell of coffee, bacon, and eggs brought everyone to the table. "Where is Beth? Is she still upstairs?" I asked.

"Don't know. We didn't see her, Mom. Maybe she took the dog out."

"Did anyone check the upstairs or basement?" asked Tony. A thorough search took place. Worried, I felt my stomach turn into knots and my face became flushed.

Tony put on his heavy coat and boots while opening the back door. "I'll look for them. They must be close to the house," he said on his way out. I could hardly close the door against the violent wind. It slammed shut.

Tony returned with snow dripping off his worried face. "Come on, boys! Bundle up and come outside with me to look for Beth. We'll have to use rope to guide us. You can't see the house fifty feet away. There's a blizzard out there. Mother's clothesline is one hundred feet long. We can use it for a guide from the house. We'll spread out fifty feet apart. Let's find them before they get frostbitten."

Tony cut and attached the ropes to railings on the back porch then tied one to each member of the search team, including himself. This would safely lead the way. The boys spread apart and followed their lifelines.

Beth, a mere one hundred feet from the house, heard Bobby calling her name. "Beth! Beth! Beth! Where are you?"

"Over here! I'm over here!" Robert followed the sound and found her and the pup under a large scrap pile of tree limbs. He yelled to Tony and Anthony, "By the brush! The brush! Come over here!" They followed the sounds until united.

Tony found Beth in a fatal position squeezed in under the lowest brush. Lady, who had snuggled under her jacket, could hardly be seen.

"I'm going to take the pooch and give her to the boys to take back to the house. I don't want you to be afraid. I'm going to pick you up and carry you back with me."

"I'm scared, Daddy."

"Don't worry. We'll be fine." When the back door burst open, my heart jumped. I welcomed the challenge of getting everyone inside, separating the laundry lines and helping to remove coats and boots.

Lady barked and ran in circles as she celebrated the rescue. Beth shivered her way to the fireplace. Drinking a hot cup of cocoa warmed her. How grateful we were no one suffered frostbite.

We took our time with breakfast while we waited for the storm to subside. The early afternoon brought a ray of sunshine. Tony and the boys shoveled the walks and driveway then scurried to the station. Cars had monitored themselves into lines at the gas pumps. Although bundled well, the boy's steamy breath could be seen in the air as they pumped gas for the customers.

Later that night, while relaxing over a casual dinner, we talked about the day Lady joined our family and the unforgettable storm we had the first night she lived with us. This will always be a special family memory.

CHAPTER 22

Zoom! Zoom! Zoom!

A silly thing. So silly it sounds childlike. Whoever heard of adults consciously repeating a word called "Zoom"? Even so, the word has become special in our family's vocabulary. In its own unique way, it helped save Tony's life.

Snowmobiling is the most popular winter sport in the Northwoods. Thousands of visitors ride the trails every year. Two hundred miles of safe marked paths are available due to the participation of local snowmobile clubs. Volunteers roam the area to remove debris and groom the trails with tractors and trucks pulling specialized equipment to smooth the snow. The air becomes saturated with the loud buzz of riding enthusiasts.

When the trails were snow-packed and ready to ride, Tony could be seen smiling with his "time to ride" call. "Zoom! Zoom! Zoom! Who wants to go?"

"Zoom! Zoom! Zoom! We do!"

Being a riding family, we have a half-dozen machines and use our "Zoom!" battle cry for the adventure. We have adopted it as our family code.

With all business closed on Sunday, I said, "I'm glad we're closed today. We can all go to the Polaris sled races in town and come back to the lake to watch the polar bear plunges," I suggested.

"Zoom, zoom, zoom," answered everybody with silly grins on their faces.

Both events raise money for two handicapped children's camps in our county. Well attended with visitors and local people, the donations are always generous.

"Better put on long underwear. We'll be outside most of the day. Put on heavy socks too," Tony said. One by one, we dressed and finished with suits, boots, helmets, and warm gloves. We were ready.

Races were held at a nearby frozen lake. Viewing areas were heavily populated and overcrowded. With no place big enough for all of us to view together, we split up to find spots for ourselves. The races ended with three girls wearing swimsuits while racing machines across the icy terrain. It gave me the chills to even imagine how cold they were. People clapped to encourage them. Fun but ridiculous fun.

After the crowds dissipated, we found one another and traveled to the polar event. We split again with a plan to meet by the heated tubs.

Hundreds of people crowded around the frozen lake where the ice had been cut out near the shoreline, opening up the water for the volunteer's jump. After they've jumped, the participants take turns warming themselves in warm water held in large metal tubs scattered, between the lake and clubhouse. The jumpers' last stop is into the building where hot showers and drinks wait them.

This year, twenty people came forward to dive into the freezing waters. They dressed in a variety of costumes and were hilarious to watch. All of a sudden, a scream interrupted the fun time.

"Stop! Get off! It's not yours! Get off! Get off! You ——!" Two men had stolen two snowmobiles in the midst of the crowd. Without hesitation, Tony yelled, "Zoom! Zoom! Zoom!" The boys heard him and answered the call to rally and ride behind him. The chase began! The thieves crossed the frozen lake going full speed. When the shorelines were reached, Tony pointed to the boys to follow one thief, and he followed the other. On and off the trails they zigzagged through the woods.

Tony caught up to his prey. The stolen machines had stopped, and the thief ran into the woods. Footprints tell all. Surrounded by silence, Tony yelled, "Zoom! Zoom! Zoom!" An answer echoed back.

The boys had stopped nearby for the same reason and heard Tony's call. Once reunited, Tony said, "I think they ran out of gas and took off to hide somewhere. It will be easy to track them in the snow. I don't think we should try it on our own. I'll stay here so we can keep tabs on where we stopped. You two go back to town and get the sheriff and lead him back. Have you got enough gas in your tanks?"

"I do, Dad. I left home filled up," Anthony answered.

"Me too. Almost full," Bob said.

"Get going then. I'll be waiting. It won't be dark for a while, so there's plenty of time. Come back as soon as you can." The boys left and returned with the sheriff.

"Only the stolen snowmobile is here. Where is Dad's?" Bob said

"Where could he be? He said he would wait for us," Anthony answered.

"Wait a minute, boys! Look at these scuffle marks in the snow. There is a small trail of blood. Something might have happened to your dad. Follow me and we'll track the freshest tracks."

With caution, the three carefully let the tracks guide them. "Zoom! Zoom! Zoom!" Bob and Anthony repeatedly hollered.

A quarter of a mile in, faint "Zooms" were heard back. "It must be Dad, hurry!" Robert said. Found tied to a tree, Tony's eyes were swollen half shut, with blood dripping from his nose and mouth. He mumbled, "You found me."

The sheriff cut Tony down and asked, "What happed?"

"The two guys who took the snowmobiles met up, snuck up behind me, and tried to tie me up. I almost beat their brains out but got tangled in their rope and fell. They kicked the —— out of me and tied me to the tree. They took off on my Arctic Cat. Put me on the back of one of your machines. I'm going after them."

"No, you're not! You're in no condition to ride. I'm taking you back," answered the sheriff. He escorted Tony and the boys back to the house.

Beth and I had returned home when they left the lake and were shocked at Tony's beat-up condition. I retrieved an ice bag to help his pain and got a bowl of hot water with washcloths to wipe and dissolve the dried blood off of his badly bruised face. His eyes were almost swollen shut and looked like two slits.

"Do you need me to call Dr. Arnold?" I asked.

"No, I just hurt. Help me clean up then get me into bed."

"At least take some aspirin for the pain," I begged.

Once in bed, Tony gave the sheriff a good description of the thieves. "They're both young, about twenty years old, and one is at least six feet tall. The other is shorter, maybe five nine or ten. They both have silver helmets. The tall one has a gray suit and the other has a dark-blue one. The short man has a front tooth missing and the tall one has long dark-brown hair. Both have writing on the backs of their suits saying, "Yonkers Heating.""

The thieves were caught and arrested by nightfall. The insane day ended on a positive note. My boys were heroes, Tony was safe, and twenty thousand dollars in donations were collected for the children's camps.

This crazy "Zoom! Zoom! Zoom!" scenario proved its worth and was a slang code used by this family indefinitely.

CHAPTER 23

Reunion

I'll never understand how this particular long-awaited day turned into one of the bloodiest accidents I ever saw. It seemed creepy the way the sand soaked up the blood. I often wonder if the devil himself tried to ruin one of the happiest days of our life. The event had been so joyous at the start.

The mail truck had stopped at our box. I stopped cleaning and routinely went out to get the mail. In the stack, a white fancy satin-like envelope stood out in the pile. It grabbed my attention and I opened it first.

An invitation from Vera and Jim for Susie's wedding laid inside the delicate invitation. The date was set for September 2, 1950. Labor Day weekend. Even though I was alone, I jumped around with excitement. *Yes, yes,* I thought while tapping my toes. I could hardly wait to tell Tony the news.

Life had gone on with Jim and Vera being gone, but even so, the fact remained that we all missed one another. Visions of Vera and I sharing our lives again made me smile to myself. *Hurry up, Tony, I can't wait to show you the invitation.*

When he did come home, I excitedly rambled on about Jim and Vera including us. "We are invited to Susie's wedding and it will be at our church. We've got to go. It's been two years since they moved away," I said.

"Of course we will go. It will be nice for Susie. She grew up in this town. Didn't Jim and Vera say at Mom's wake they would stop by and see us some time?" answered Tony.

"They did. It's been a while, so maybe I should call Vera to see how they are."

"I saw Jim in town the other day and he looked great. I asked him how they all were, and he said everyone is fine. He told me his station is for sale."

"How come you didn't mention it?" I asked.

"Guess I forgot. He's still a hardworking guy and he's looking for another business."

"I'm going to call Vera. I'll invite them for dinner Sunday."

Vera's voice sounded good to me over the phone. We talked for the better part of an hour.

"I stayed with Jim because I really love him. We're okay now. He quit drinking and got himself involved with a group called Alcoholics Anonymous. One of the men who works for us goes. He invited Jim to attend a meeting with him. Jim wanted desperately to stop his addiction and went. The rest is history. This is what he needed. I also go to an AA group meeting for families of alcoholics. Jim is his old sweet self again."

"I've heard of AA and all of the amazing things they do. I'm so glad it worked for you two. Tony and I have missed you both. We've been busy out of our minds, like always, but we can definitely make time to get together with you two and the kids. How about coming over for dinner Sunday?" I asked.

"Sound's good. If we come to Granite for church Sunday, we could come to your house afterward. Will this time frame work?"

"I'm so happy you'll come. I look forward to Sunday," I answered.

Jim, Vera, and their children arrived for church early. We got there ahead of time too because Tony was ushering that day.

I looked up from our pew and there they were. I jumped up and ran to Vera. We hugged like two matching puzzle pieces. Tears flowed. Tony and Jim shook hands with smiles bright enough to light up a Christmas tree. The children could be heard giggling in the back of the church. It seemed like we had been frozen in time and no time had been lost.

It took some effort to quiet down and put our reunion aside during church service, but we did. It seemed as though the sermon subject had been chosen just for us. Pastor Johnson spoke on the value of relationships, both with our friends and our Lord Jesus. Coincidence?

Dinner slowly cooked in the oven while we were in church. Beth had helped me set the table and gather extra chairs. Things were ready beforehand. When we arrived home, we followed one another directly into the dining room. Our appetites were ravenous. We served the meal in record time.

"I remember your kitchen just as it is. It hasn't changed a bit. Everything is just as I remembered it. I love it," Vera said.

"You're right, it's still the same, except maybe for the curtains. Did you live in Granite when I made them?" I asked.

"Sure, I remember when you made them. When the guys went to Canada on their duck hunting trip, you sewed the curtains and I finished my quilt." Who would have thought such boring girl talk would be exciting? We were all happy being together again.

We sat around the table and updated one another on the past two years. The children went outside to play baseball. During our conversation, Jim looked at Tony and me and said, "I want to apologize for the way I behaved at Clare's wedding. I'm really sorry. Can you two forgive me?"

"Of course," Tony said as he stood to shake Jim's hand.

"Nothing ever happened as far as I'm concerned," I answered. Our smiles were broad enough to cross the continent. We continued to share updates and talked about Susie's wedding. Our silly dogs were a hot topic. They had a German shepherd named Sport, and we had Lady. Canine stories were always good for laughs.

Jim told us he had a buyer for his station. "I'm uncertain what I'll be doing after it's gone, but I have a few ideas. Just no definite plans yet," he said.

Suddenly, the back door slammed, almost off its hinges. "Dad, Bobby's teeth are gone. He's bleeding all over. He got hit in the face with the bat. He's bleeding bad. Come on right away," Anthony said.

"Where is he?"

"Down by the lake." The four of us ran. I grabbed a pile of towels on my way out. Anthony led the way.

Bobby sat in a pool of blood slowly saturating the sand. Even though tears ran down his cheeks, he felt too grown to cry. After all, when you're fourteen, you're almost a man. He looked up at us. His face looked like it had been hit by a train. His disfigured nose and mouth were pushed back and swollen. Blood continued to drip from his mouth. You could see where his four front teeth had been ripped away. Loose flesh hung down from his gums. Unable to talk, he stared at us while I wrapped towels around his shoulders to catch his blood. The bleeding slowed down but still occasionally dripped down his chin.

"It's okay, Bob, you're going to be all right," Tony said while he stared at his son and tried to evaluate the injury.

"Do any of you know where his teeth went?" I asked. Bob and the other children shook their heads from side to side and mumbled "no."

"I'm going to look. If we can find them, maybe they can be transplanted." Everyone helped me search. We could not find them. In all probability, the sand had gobbled them.

"Bob, we need to take you up to the house. Can you walk?" Tony asked.

With his eyes half shut, he managed to say, "Okay."

Tony put his arm around Bob for support and started the incline. Bob's knees caved, and Jim had walked alongside them to assist. Together, they got him up the hill and into the house.

"I don't know if we should put ice on his face or not. I think we should take him to the hospital for treatment. This is a nasty injury," I said.

"Let's not take any chances and do the wrong thing. Can you help me take him in, Jim?" Tony asked.

"Absolutely."

I went with them while Vera stayed back at the house and managed the children and the dogs. Everyone was anxious and visibly shaken after the accident. The dogs paced back and forth. The kids repeated the story over and over again, shifting the blame from one to the other.

"It's time you all quiet down. Sometimes accidents happen and they're not really anyone's fault. They just happen. You all know none of you would hurt Bobby on purpose. He's going to be all right, and if you really want to help, you can do that by doing what your mom and dad ask you to do. Start by being patient until they return," Vera said. Agreeing with her, they responded and waited quietly.

After emergency treatment, the family members returned. Although very uncomfortable, Bobby would be all right. Stitches were used and the bleeding stopped. He would need four artificial implanted teeth and facial surgery.

"Here we go, Vera. Just like old times. I am so glad you were here today," I said.

"It does feel right, doesn't it? I'm glad we were here too."

Jim and Vera had over an hour traveling time back to Rice Lake. "We have to leave now to go home. Tomorrow is a workday. When you're near our place, stop by and we'll do the same," Jim said.

"Thanks for your help. When trouble hits, there is nothing better than to have true friends around to help you," answered Tony.

"Guess you could say we had an unusual reunion of some sort today. Let's keep it going," I said.

"We will. See you later," they said as they pulled out of our drive.

CHAPTER 24

Mr. Negative

For good reason, we felt like someone had taken our community, homes, and businesses, put them all in a fishbowl, and shook them, letting pieces fall into place where they landed. Who would have thought ten years back that Granite would fashion new faces in old places? Sometimes change is good. The trick is to be flexible and let things happen in their own natural way.

Vera and Jim frequently stopped by the station and our house when in our area. We did the same. Our dogs, Sport and Lady, became great friends. The children played every game invented by man. We enjoyed being together again.

Susie's wedding took place as planned in September. She and her husband, Mark, preferred the small, intimate wedding in the parsonage. Their family and closest friends were present. After the ceremony, guests were invited to a buffet-style dinner served in the church basement. Most everyone there knew one another. The simplicity of the event made it beautiful.

While chatting, Mr. Powdy from the general hardware store announced his retirement. "It's time for me to move on. I've had the store from the first day it opened its doors forty-five years ago. I'm too darn full of arthritis to bother with it anymore. Once it's gone, I want to move to a warmer climate. These long winters are hard on me," he said. We were all surprised.

"Are you really ready to sell your place?" answered Jim.

"Yep! As soon as I can."

"I've got my station in Rice Lake for sale. It's possible I have a buyer as we speak. I've been undecided about what I should do income-wise after it's sold. Don't you have a residence on the lot behind the store?"

"Yes, the house is almost forty years old. We built it after we opened the business and raised our family in it. I plan on selling the business and the house in a package deal, if I can."

"I'm interested. I'll talk with Vera about it, then I'll stop in. I have a lot of questions," answered Jim. If this arrangement moved forward, circumstances would be favorable for everyone involved.

After Susie's wedding reception, we helped Jim and Vera clean up the buffet tables in the fellowship hall. "I'm kind of excited about the possibility of you moving back to Granite. Gosh! It would be like it used to be for the four of us. The store is close to the station. We could see each other in town a lot," I giggled.

"Wouldn't it be exciting if it all works out?" answered Vera.

"Let us know how things go. We're glad to help if needed," Tony said.

We loaded the trash and took it to the town dump. When we finished, we decided to go home. It had been a long day, leaving us with plenty to think about.

Vera and Jim both liked the idea of having a hardware business with a home on the premises. Life would be less complicated for them with this arrangement.

"Jim, I could be of so much more help to you if we live close to the store," said Vera.

"It would be easier for me too. I think I could get the hang of it. I'll know tomorrow if the deal went through on the sale of the station. If it did, we can meet with Mr. Powdy and ask some more questions. Let's write them down as we think of them," Jim said.

The sale went through and Vera and Jim met with Mr. Powdy. Questions were asked on both sides. After an agreement took place, Jim and Vera purchased the property. The deal closed the first week in October. Our dear friends kept us updated the day of their closing. We preplanned to meet in town for lunch after they finished. The new homeowners strutted into the restaurant with success written all over their faces.

"Congratulations! You'll do really well with the store. I know you will. It's the oldest and most established business in town," Tony said.

Vera and I hugged with smiles from here to Lake Michigan. "Can you believe this? We're practically neighbors again! Our businesses are a block apart and our houses just a mile apart," I said.

"I know. Who would ever think we'd end up so close to one another again? It's almost too good to be true," said Vera. It took a lot of self-control not to dance around the floor to celebrate.

"The closing went smoothly. Good God, I hope we make it," said Jim.

"Are you kidding? The store is a sure bet! You can't help but make it," Tony laughed.

Mr. Powdy introduced Jim to the hardware business while waiting for their deal to close. Well-informed, Jim took over right after the final papers were signed. Packed and ready to leave, Mr. Powdy said goodbye to Granite and moved away the following weekend. Jim and Vera followed with their move. We helped them and finished the same day.

"The way things fell into place for you two, it's obvious this is supposed to be. There isn't much left on the truck. Let's wrap it up," Tony said.

"We have one bedframe still on board. After we move it, let's take a swim. I'm dripping with sweat. The lake is still warm and the public beach is just a block from here. Let's go there," Jim said.

This sounded appealing, so when we were done unpacking the truck, we ran full speed to the beach. We laughed so hard we almost tripped over one another. Tony and Jim kicked their shoes off before they hit the water, fully clothed. Along came Vera and I, who were just as crazy. We jumped in too.

When we cooled down, we came out and proceeded, dripping wet, back to Jim and Vera's place.

"Are we all nuts? Glad the kids didn't see us," Jim said.

"Maybe they did. You can see the beach from the station. The boys are working there now." Tony laughed.

"Oh well! We've got good reason to celebrate, right?" Jim said with a smile as big as the lake alongside him.

The day had gotten warmer than usual for this time of year and our clothes dried quickly. We walked back to Jim's place, where we quenched our thirst with his garden hose. After our goodbyes, we headed home.

"Isn't it amazing how good things can happen all on their own?" I said.

"Yep, and sometimes things turn out bad, no matter what you do."

"Come on, Mr. Negative. You're usually the positive one around here. What gives?" I said.

"Had some chest pains after the swim. They're gone now."

My face dropped in concern as I squinted my eyes into a frowning look. "Are you sure you're all right? Why didn't you say something?" I asked.

"I'm okay now. I didn't realize it at first. The pains took me by surprise."

"You better mention it to Dr. Arnold. If you don't tell her, I will." Pulling on Tony's arm gave me balance to reach up and kiss him on the cheek.

"You've got to take care of yourself, honey. Promise me you'll tell the doctor," I said.

"Okay."

CHAPTER 25

A Newfound Freedom

I hit a tree at 40 mph, flirting with death. The impact jerked my body and pushed my face against the wheel. Worse yet, Vera was knocked out by the crash and scared me to death. What a disaster!

The day had run smoothly until Vera and I decided to teach me to drive. With Jim and Vera's home close and everyone working nearby, Jim and Tony ran back and forth from each other's businesses daily. When Jim needed new shelves in his store, Tony made and installed them. If Tony got behind on mechanical work, Jim would come to the station and manage the driveway and office so Tony could work uninterrupted. Like in the past, they worked together like the sway of tree branches in the wind.

Their boys and ours resumed sports together as though they had never stopped playing and Vera and I shared household adventures as always.

Jim and Tony took a few days off to hunt. While gone, I asked Vera to help me learn to drive. "Everyone in our family drives except Beth and me. Being the only adult who doesn't drive leaves me feeling useless. No one ever seems to have time to practice with me. Would you go out with me? I would love to surprise Tony by learning to drive."

"Gosh! You're right. I'll help you. Let's go to the park Sunday afternoon and practice. With the boys away hunting, they won't know about it."

Sunday after church, I borrowed Bobby's car. Vera drove us over to the park and parked on a back road. "Okay, you take the wheel now," she said.

Finally seated in the driver's seat, my expectations soared.

"Go ahead. Drive around the paved roads," Vera instructed. Turning the key started the car.

"Now what?" I asked.

"Just go ahead and drive."

I looked out the windshield, moved my right foot, and pressed down to go forward. But a horrible thing happened. I pushed firmly down on the gas pedal, not the brake. The car jumped, roared, and sped off the road, straight into a big old birch tree. With the tremendous impact, Vera hit her head on the dashboard, knocking her out. My face and chest hit the steering wheel.

"Vera, oh my god! You're dead," I screamed. I yelled for help. "Help, help, somebody help!" Vera regained consciousness.

"Are you all right?"

"My head hurts. So does my knee. What happened?"

"The car hit a tree. It's my fault. Please forgive me for hurting you." I started to cry.

"It's okay. Just get me home. I know it's an accident. I thought you knew the basics and just needed practice."

By this time, the town already knew I hit a tree. Mrs. Webber was nearby when the accident occurred, and she saw our sons involved in basketball on the other side of the park. She drove quickly to fetch them. They didn't lose any time coming to our rescue.

"Mom, are you guys okay? What happened to my car?" asked Bobby. We stumbled through our explanation.

"We will take you two home and then come back and tow the car to the station," Anthony said.

"Good idea. Take Vera home first. She feels terrible. Should we call Dr. Arnold?" I asked.

"My head hurts something awful, but I'm all right. Don't worry about it. You got banged up too. I'll see you tomorrow."

The boys had been a big help when they took matters into their own hands. After Tony returned, the shocked look on his face when he saw the damaged car reminded me of someone who found their car destroyed in a parking lot.

"Can't you all behave when I'm gone? Glad no one got seriously injured. Next time you want to drive, let me take you. We'll try and fix Bobby's car tomorrow if we can," Tony said.

The next day, when I saw my image in the mirror, I hardly recognized myself. Overnight, my face had become black and blue. It made me look like an animal. Both eyes were circled in purple and blue. My chest had become badly bruised too.

It became urgent for me to check on Vera. When she opened her front door to let me in, I found her face discolored too. "How is your head and leg?" I asked.

"I'm all right. Look at our faces," she said while she tried not to laugh. "You have a raccoon face."

"A raccoon? So do you! Aren't we goofy lookin'?" Silly and laughing, we called each other "raccoon face."

The front end of Bobby's car looked like a squashed watermelon in a field. We thought it best to replace the whole car.

"There's a customer who wants to sell one of his cars. I'll take Bobby to look at it. I know the car and it's in good condition. If Bobby likes it, we could buy it to replace his. What do you think?" Tony asked.

"When it comes to cars, count me out. Don't know anything about them. So sorry Bob's car is ruined. You pick out the replacement for me. You take the reins on this one."

Bob liked the car. We bought it and took the damaged vehicle to a junkyard.

"When do you want to start some driving lessons?" asked Tony.

"Let's wait for a while. The tree accident is fresh in my mind. I don't want to learn right now. It is said that your spouse should not teach you to drive, but we can try and see how it goes, maybe next month."

A few weeks later, we tried. With patience and mutual respect for each other, we somehow managed to practice twice a week.

Before winter began, I took a driver's test and passed. Amazing! Being able to drive was a newfound freedom for me. Why did I wait so long to learn?

CHAPTER 26

Kidnapped

Watching Beth sit alongside Lady for hours should have been a clue to what her life's calling would be. Gently, she held the badly mauled pup's head and offered her water, kept her warm, and carried her when she had to go outside. Beth's gentle touch and patience marked her as a nurse of the future.

If we had stayed home that evening, I wonder if we could have stopped the catastrophe.

Being married twenty-five years is a milestone in any marriage. Tony remembered ours.

"Babe, it's been awhile since we've gone out for dinner. Let's go to Eagle River for a good steak and celebrate our twenty-fifth anniversary," Tony said.

"You're right, we should. But I'd rather buy steaks and eat at home."

"Twenty-five years is a long time. I want to do something special. Let's go to the Runabout Supper Club. Their dinner organ music is abeyance at its finest. How about Saturday night?"

"You're right. This is a once-in-a-lifetime anniversary," I answered. When we left, I said, "You boys watch after Beth. We'll be gone a while, so stay in with her tonight. When we're out of the area, it's reassuring to know you're all safe at home, okay?" I said.

"Sure, Mom, we'll be fine. You and Dad have a good time, and we'll just go on to bed if you're out late. We weren't going anywhere anyway," Anthony answered.

I had to admit, being dressed up in a pretty dress with high heels and party-style jewelry did make the evening feel special. When we were parking the car at the restaurant, we saw Jim and Vera's car parked close. I pointed it out to Tony and said, "They'll be surprised to see us. Help me look for them."

Once inside, Tony asked the hostess to lead us to the group in the back room. Confused by his question, I followed him and I began to see people we knew. The decorated room had silver ribbons and bells and looked festive. Everyone yelled, "Surprise!"

Shocked, my mouth fell open. Having not suspected anything about the surprise, I was totally overwhelmed. How did everyone keep the secret? I covered my face with my hands. Tony stood beside me with a boyish grin. I grabbed onto him and gave him the biggest hug ever.

"Tony! You devil you! You knew all along." I turned toward Jim and Vera and shook my finger at them. "You little sneaks. You knew too, didn't you?"

"Yep, we sure did. Happy anniversary!" Vera said.

We partied and danced until everyone ran out of steam. Vera and Jim helped carry the leftover cake and gifts to the car. "We're going to come over and help you eat this leftover cake tomorrow," said Jim as he closed his car door.

"You betcha!" we hollered as we pulled away.

A full moon lit the roads. Tony drove slowly to avoid hitting any deer. They were out on the dark roads more than usual. The extra time gave me a chance to unwind.

"I'll never forget tonight. I still can't believe it. I never picked up on the surprise," I said.

"There were times I almost gave it away. If you hadn't been distracted, you would have figured it out. It's not every day someone fools you. Fortunately, it went right over your head," Tony said.

"I love you! You're the best!" We approached the house and driveway. We could see all of the inside and outside lights were on.

"What are all these lights on for?" Tony said. The children were still up. Beth ran to us crying while they all started to talk at the same time.

"Lady is gone. Some animal got her."

"Beth took the dog outside in the dark. Something grabbed Lady. She yelped and squealed while being dragged away. Beth screamed and Anthony and I ran outside and couldn't see anything. We turned on the yard lights and tried to find her. We didn't know what else to do," Bobby rambled.

We assured the children they had done well. "I'll go outside and see if I can find any sign of Lady. You boys come with me," Tony said. With bright flashlights, they searched around the house.

"Look, Dad! There are prints over here. They're not deer," Anthony said. Tony inspected them.

"There's a few mountain lions still around here, and they roam around at night. I wouldn't be surprised if these prints belong to one of them. Don't tell Beth because we don't know for sure. We'll get up early and follow the trail. Maybe we'll find Lady."

We went to bed, but sleep escaped us. Beth, unsettled, could be heard crying. She loved her dog with all her heart.

As planned, Tony and the boys rose early, took their shotguns, and left for the search. They started where the tracks began.

"The scuffle marks are definitely mountain lion. I'd guess about two hundred pounds. The small paw marks could be Lady's. This might be where it grabbed her. Here's a little blood. I'll lead, you two follow," Tony said.

Quietly, they moved along a telltale path deep into the woods. Tony stopped abruptly as he moved his left hand to signal a stop then forwarded it to his lips to imply "quiet." A hissing growl penetrated the silence around them. Their eyes searched for the threat and found it. A spotted mountain lion, with glaring eyes and clinched jaw, sat perched on a large tree limb, some forty feet away. It dared them to take another step.

Deliberate and confident, Tony signaled the boys to raise their guns while very slowly he advanced toward the target. Without hesitation, they fired their guns as the monster leaped toward them.

The animal fell within inches of Tony's feet. Its tail touched his boot. Rightfully so, the vicious scavenger lay on the sandy ground, dead.

"I'll call the D&R to report the kill after we're done. We still need to find Lady," Tony said. Together they regrouped and resumed focus.

Blood appeared on the trail. It led them to a fallen decayed tree trunk. Lady laid motionless, close to the bark.

"I see her chest barely moving. She is struggling to breathe," Bobby said.

"You're right. She's tore up and very weak. Let's get her back home and to the vet. Maybe Lady's got a chance," Tony said. Wrapping Lady in his flannel shirt, they were home within minutes.

The family rushed Lady to the animal hospital. While being treated and stitched, she didn't regain consciousness. When she was discharged to home, her life hung in the balance of time. Every available moment away from school, Beth spent with her precious dog. Slowly, over a two-week period, and with Beth's loving care, Lady gained most of her strength back while her torn coat healed.

There was no doubt about it, even though she was kidnapped and mauled by a beast, our spunky family pet survived.

CHAPTER 27

The Nag

The snow came down, landed on my face, and melted. The night so quiet, you could hear your breath as it climbed the stairway to the sky. A beautiful scene, perfect for Christmas Eve. Why, then, did this holy night have to be different?

Special plans had been made for a family reunion to be held at our house. David called from Chicago to assure us he would come home for Christmas and would bring a young lady named June. They planned to marry next summer. It was time to meet our new daughter-in-law-to-be.

"If all goes well, between now and the holidays, we'll have all of our children here for Christmas dinner. It has been a while since we sat down together. I'll make your favorite apple pie," I said.

"Sit down here for a minute. I want to talk to you. I think we should buy a pool table. Jim and I discussed it and he said he could order it through his store at a discount. It can be delivered and put downstairs. I want to order one now to ensure we have it in time for the holidays. Everyone will enjoy it," Tony said.

"I like the idea! The boys especially will like it. Vera suggested I pick out Christmas gifts from their store catalogs at a discounted price too. Before you order, I'd like to paint the downstairs walls. It's so drab down there. Let's paint them a light sand color. The contrast will look nice with our brown furniture."

"Sounds good. If the boys help, we could do it in one weekend. If you can get things out of the way during the week, we'll paint next Sunday."

The basement looked larger with a light color. With the furniture pushed aside, there was adequate space left for the table. Tony put a ceiling light fixture overhead where the table would stand. Perfect! The room beckoned us to play and the pool table came in time for our reunion.

Clare and her husband, Rodger, were the first to arrive on the afternoon of Christmas Eve day. They announced exciting news about the expectant arrival of their baby next June. The idea of being a grandmother took me by surprise.

"This is wonderful! Wow! I can't wait for you to tell Dad," I said.

David and June made entrance at dinnertime. With hugs and laughter, we celebrated our reunion.

"Dad should be home any minute with the boys. You know how busy he gets in the winter. We have a pool table downstairs. Check it out while I try and keep dinner warm.

Suddenly, Tony kicked open the backdoor and screamed, "Help me! I'm having a —— heart attack!" His fist desperately clutched his chest. His eyes glared. I stared all of ten seconds. I knew Tony only swore when things were horrific and unbearable.

"Oh, Tony!" I whispered, rushing to his side. The commotion called the family to the kitchen.

"Come on, Dad, let me take you to the hospital," Dave pleaded. Rigid from pain, Tony collapsed. June, being a nurse, stepped in and attended to Tony's needs. After checking his vitals, she advised us to call for an ambulance. Twenty minutes later it arrived.

Rodger drove the family in our car and we followed the ambulance to the hospital. Treatment was given in the emergency room and was shortly followed with admittance to the hospital. Tests relayed that Tony did have a heart attack.

Once his pain had diminished, Tony said, "I'm all right. I don't want you to spend Christmas Eve here. Go home and celebrate. The doctor said I could possibly be released in a couple of days. Call Jim to help you manage the station. I'll be home as soon as I can."

I didn't want to leave, but Tony insisted. After an emotional departure with hugs and hand squeezing, we parted.

Our gifts for one another had been placed under the tree. After a warmed-over dinner, we sat in the front room and opened the gifts. Emotions ran high as we laughed and oohed and aahed while opening each present wrapped in holiday paper. It didn't feel the same with Tony gone. We all missed him.

Still worried, there were tears in my eyes. I was not going to break down in front of the children, I told myself. We need to be strong.

I called Jim and explained what had taken place and asked him if he could help run things until Tony came back. Of course, he knew how and gladly stepped right up. It gave us peace to know we could count on him.

The family enjoyed playing pool. Between hospital visits, the game table seemed to be constantly in use.

After Christmas, Dave and Clare needed to travel back to their homes because of their jobs.

"I hate to leave you here without us. You will have your hands full when Dad comes home," Clare said.

"I'll be all right. I can drive and things will be manageable."

"June and I will come back as soon as we can," Dave said.

I had found June to be delightful, and I thanked Dave's bride-to-be for all of her help. They announced their wedding date of July 25, 1952.

"We'll be there, I am sure. Dad's better already," I said.

Clare and Rodger did not have the opportunity to tell Tony about their baby. They decided to stop at the hospital to tell him before they left town. I went with them.

After a hug, Clare said, "Dad, Rodger and I have a surprise for you. You're going to be a grandfather. We're having a baby next June."

"Me? I'm going to be a grandfather? I can't believe it. I'm not old enough. What do you say about this, Grandmother?" He laughed. His big smiled made it obvious that he was happy about the news.

"You have another reason to get better now. The baby is due in the spring and Dave and June's wedding is in July. You're going to be busy, Grandpa," I teased.

Tony came home two days after the children left. Dr. Arnold said Tony was very fortunate and didn't have a lot of heart damage.

"Consider this attack a warning. You need to change your life-style if you want to survive. Get more rest and eat healthy," she said.

When Tony came home, he appeared weaker than normal. He napped a lot and picked at his food. This wasn't like him. Soon, I could see his strength return as he ate larger portions and stayed awake longer.

Jim and Vera came over often to check on us. We told them about our expected grandchild.

"I didn't tell you because Sue is waiting for a test to verify her pregnancy, but we're going to become grandparents too." Vera laughed.

"We sure do things together, don't we? When is Susie due?" I asked.

"June."

"So is Clare. Here we go again." We couldn't have planned things any better than they were. The girls' expected dates were two days apart. Vera and I talked grandma talk. Jim and Tony discussed station business. Jim did a good job helping us run things while Tony recovered. If he hadn't, the boys and I couldn't have managed things as well on our own.

The men in our family wore the felt on top of the pool table thin from playing daily. Sometimes Vera and I joined them. To keep Tony's mind busy during recovery, the four of us played pinochle two nights a week. We had fun and enjoyed every game.

Recovering more quickly than expected, Tony resumed all activities in six weeks.

One night, I lingered over dinner and said, "I want you to be honest with me about how you're feeling. I know you don't want to complain, but it is important you take care of yourself. A heart attack is nothing to forget about. Maybe you can cut your work hours a little bit and get more rest?"

"I do get tired sometimes and fall asleep in my chair reading the paper. I'll work on the idea of getting more rest."

"You were blessed this time, but maybe you won't be again. Promise me you'll try," I pleaded.

"I don't want to miss Dave's wedding. I'll arrange something. Maybe I could hire someone part-time and cut my hours in half. After all, I am going to be a grandpa."

"I'm so glad you're all right. I couldn't bear it if anything happened to you," I said as I walked over to him for a big hug. "I'm going to nag you about this until you change your hours."

"Nag, nag, nag. I love you, you beautiful nag."

CHAPTER 28

For the Birds

I never thought I would see the day when I would run around the yard with a rake, chasing wild turkeys. They scattered so fast, some of their feathers flew up in the air and spiraled down. My guess would have been a count of more than twenty. We were shocked, upon our return from David and June's wedding, to find these mean-spirited monsters.

Our visit to Sandwich, Illinois, for the affair later became one of our favorite trips. Vera, Jim, and their family were invited too. We traveled together in separate cars and stopped only for gas and meals.

Seldom having eaten in restaurants, the children considered the many food choices to be a special event. They studied their menus and their orders radically differed.

Approaching Chicago, Tony suggested, "We better take out-lying roads. This city is massive and we might get lost. Traffic is congested."

"Our hearts are set on seeing skyscrapers. Will we see any on the backroads?" I asked.

"I don't know. Things have changed since I lived here. If we miss them going in, we can look for them on our way out."

The children stared out the windows, taking in the scenery. Multiple stoplights, houses close together, carpet-like green lawns, and stores everywhere. The landscape fascinated me too.

When we arrived, June's family welcomed us wholeheartedly and invited us to be their guests. The ten of us, we felt, would be an imposition. A motel nearby seemed adequate. We gracefully declined and Tony and Jim reserved adjoining rooms. Our youngsters were amazed at the long carpeted corridors and multiple doors with room numbers on them. They had never stayed in a motel before. The realization that beds were in each room astonished them. Would this many people sleep here overnight?

The wedding ceremony took place in June's church. We watched our firstborn take the hand of his lovely bride, who would be his treasure for the rest of his life. Tony and I felt he had made a good choice.

The reception followed outdoors in June's backyard. A large tent covered half of the area with chairs and tables underneath. Guests were protected from the elements. All of us had a good time in the bride's garden. We satisfied our taste buds with elegant Swedish delicacies, served buffet-style. We sang and danced to music provided by a record player and speakers. Music selections were familiar, making it easier for the children to join us.

June and David left on their honeymoon after the buffet and we departed shortly after dark. It had been a long day, the hotel beds felt cozy. While traveling the area, we had seen country roads and small towns. Mile after mile of flat farmland had seemed vacant. There were no trees and an absence of hills. Where were the woods?

"Can we drive close to the Chicago limits and see big tall buildings?" I asked.

"Sure, we'll stay longer. I'll take you downtown to the Museum of Science and Industry and the Art Institute. I'll ask Jim and Vera to join us." Vera and Jim agreed to go.

"Did you really grow up here? Show us your house, Dad."

"I did. I lived on Chicago's north side. Where I lived is long gone. When we leave to go home, I'll drive along Lake Michigan's shoreline. You will see how big the lake is."

For two days, we "oohed" and "aahed" as we observed the enormous city. Jim, Vera, and their children accompanied us everywhere. Before we left to go home, we said goodbye to June's family.

The trip back seemed noisy as we continually talked about all we had seen. When we approached the north part of Wisconsin, the scenery changed. Woods and evergreens surrounded us. Tony sang

"America the Beautiful." We didn't hesitate to join in with loud singing. I wondered if anyone outside could hear us. We sounded terrible.

When we reached Granite, Jim and Vera exited our caravan. We headed toward home and pulled into our driveway.

"Oh my god! Look at all the turkeys on our roof," I screamed. Jumping out of the car, we gazed in disbelief.

"Shoo! Shoo! Get out of here," Tony yelled.

"Shoo, you dirty birds. Shoo!" the rest of us shouted.

There were about three-dozen turkeys. We startled them and feathers flew as some took flight. A few attempted to drop to the porch and to the ground. All of them gobbled in a frenzy. A half dozen of them were brazen and lunged toward us, but their gobbler's feet couldn't run as fast as ours.

Tony picked up a rake from the yard and charged back. We joined him. Running scared, they wobbled back and forth and tried to outrun us. Convinced they'd lose the battle, the red gobbler pests headed into the woods.

"You and the kids go on in the house. I'm going to put the ladder up to the roof and inspect it for damage. Those darn turkeys peck at the fine gravel on the shingles, and some shingles may have torn off. I don't want any roof leaks."

The children helped with the luggage and unpacked. Tony joined us within the hour.

"How does it look up there? Any shingles gone?" I asked.

"Six or eight. I'll have to fix them tomorrow before we get rain, or we'll get leak for sure."

"Isn't it hard for you to be up on the roof? I'm afraid you'll fall. After all, you were a sick man four months ago."

"I'm okay. It's not too big of a job," Tony said.

"The kids go to school tomorrow, so the boys can't help. I'll give you a hand."

Once we were up on the roof, Tony fixed it then spotted a tree down across our backyard. A pile of sawdust lay around a trunk stump.

"While we were gone, a foliated woodpecker took the big maple down. What gives?" Tony asked.

"I don't know, honey. All I can say is, 'It's for the birds.'"

CHAPTER 29

Family Unity

The phone rang. I was irritated. Getting dinner started on time is a must. Now what? Interrupted again? Sometimes I can't get things done around here. Grumble, grumble. I'm Crabby!

"Hi, Mom. I just came from Dr. Arnold's office. You'll never guess what she told me. I'm carrying twins," said Clare.

"Oh my gosh! Are you sure?"

"Yes, there are two heartbeats."

"Twins run on my side of the family. What a surprise. Dad's working on a cradle for you. Now he'll have to make two."

I have to admit, my nasty disposition turned to joy. What could be more wonderful than two precious babies? I could hardly wait until Tony came home to tell him the exciting news.

"Hey there, Grandpa. Guess what? Clare called, and she and Rodger are having twins. Can you imagine?"

"Really? Who would have thought? Guess I better hurry with the baby's bed and make another." We were happy about the news and shared it with friends. We boasted. Vera and I had fun planning for our grandchildren. We made things and bought baby items. Her Susie and my Clare were due so close together. We made things fun as we tried to predict who might give birth first and who would become grandma the quickest.

One day, Rodger called. He hesitated a moment, and when I heard the sorrowful tone of his voice, I shuddered.

"I'm calling you from the hospital. Clare miscarried."

"Oh no! What happened?"

"We don't know. She went into labor. It couldn't be stopped. We're devastated," Rodger cried.

"What can we do to help?" I asked as tears streamed down my cheeks.

"Can you and Dad come to the hospital?"

"Yes, we'll be there as soon as we can."

The children sought medical help seventy miles away from Granite. Tony and I got there within the hour. Rodger waited at the hospital entrance for us.

"I'm glad you could come," Rodger said. His eyes were dazed and red from crying, which gave us the immediate message that support was needed. As we walked to Clare's room, he said, "Can we stop here in the waiting room for a bit?"

"Sure."

"Clare is in shock and barely talks straight. She cries with every word. I told her things will be all right, that we can plan a family again later. I know she will feel better if she sees and talks with you. Help me help her."

"Of course! We're sorry this happened. Clare is strong, she'll be all right. Having always been daddy's little girl, we should let Tony visit with her first."

Tony found his once-baby-princess smothered in sorrow. Putting up her arms, she signaled him to come close. When Tony's strong daddy arms embraced her, she wept uncontrollably.

"It's going to be all right, honey. Everything is going to be all right. Pull yourself together for Rodger. He's worried sick about you. You're young and you two can still have a family. We don't know why the babies had to go home so early, but God does. Trust Him. He promises us He's working for our good in all circumstances," Tony said.

"You're right, Daddy. I know you are, but I feel so defeated. This is hard. I need some time."

"Good girl."

Clare called for Rodger and I to join them. We talked about Clare going home.

"When you are discharged, I'll stay with you for a while so Rodger can get back to work," I said.

"I would appreciate that. If I know she is in good hands, I can leave her without worry. I don't want her to be alone until I'm sure she's back to herself. My family can help too."

Five days later, Clare came home. Both families supported the children until they recovered. Optimistically, Tony and I put all of the baby things in the attic, as storing them for the future seemed logical.

When Clare went in for a six-week checkup, she got a surprise beyond her belief.

"I'm hearing a heartbeat. You're still pregnant," said Dr. Arnold.

"Are you sure? How can this be?"

"Even though you miscarried, one of the babies survived. It is very rare, but sometimes it happens."

"Oh my gosh! I can't wait to tell Rodger."

When Rodger came home, Clare ran to the door and blurted, "I know it sounds crazy but I am still pregnant. One twin passed, the other survived. There is no way to know the condition of this one, but it's a miracle baby. I am just scared something might happen again."

"No way! Are you telling me the truth?"

"Yes! You're all right with this, aren't you?"

"It is hard to believe," Rodger answered.

After accepting the idea, they were afraid to be happy. "I want to plan for the baby but I can't. What if I miscarry again?" said Clare.

"What if you don't? Maybe everything's okay. Let's not pick a name until it's born," Rodger suggested.

As time passed, their hearts gave way to looking forward to being parents. The news about the baby spread fast. Tony and I talked positive about our little grandchild, whose life hung desperately from day-to-day.

"Dad and I would like to buy a buggy for the baby. We think you two should pick it out."

"Really? There is one Rodger and I like, but we thought we would wait to see how things go before we bought one." With pretend confidence, I assured them all would be well. Perhaps talking positive would make it so.

Vera and I still suffered from "grandmother's" joy. We chatted about the babies' needs whenever we were together.

Decoration Day arrived. Both Susie and Clare looked ready to deliver. They walked as though they were carrying barrels.

"Won't be long now. Susie picked out names for the baby. I can hardly stand the wait," giggled Vera.

"No one ever told me it would be this hard to be a grandmother. I wake up every night thinking I might get another call," I whined.

"Let's hope not."

Rodger called us at seven the next morning. "Clare and I are at the hospital. She just delivered a seven-pound boy. He is full-term, but he's not doing well. The doctor said he must have lost ground during the miscarriage because his lungs are not fully developed. He can't breathe very easily, and he is hooked up to machines."

"I am so sorry, honey."

"I'll call you back when I know more," Rodger said.

"We'll wait to hear from you."

Later, Rodger asked us to come to the hospital. The children named their son Steven and spoke of him by name.

"Steven is fighting hard, Mom. I can't bring you in the unit where he is, so we'll have to sit here and wait together," said Clare.

"Fine, we'll be here for as long as you need us."

Tony took Rodger out for supper while I stayed with Clare. Time dragged on. Knowing her sweet baby fought for every breath, it made the wait unbearable.

"This can't be. Steven has got to be okay. He's so tiny. Mom, what can I do?"

"There's nothing we can do except wait and trust the good Lord."

"Trust Him? I hate Him! How can He do this to my little boy? I hate Him!" she sobbed as she leaned into my arms.

"Okay, honey! It's okay."

Clare sat on the couch in the waiting area until her crying subsided. Rodger and Tony returned. Clare had become exhausted. She blinked her eyes and stared into space.

"Let Rodger take you back to your room. You need to rest. Dad and I will stay here." After hugging us, she took Rodger's hand and went back to her room to lie down and rest. Rodger stayed with her until she fell asleep then rejoined us.

Dr. Arnold walked into the room to speak with Rodger.

"Things are not going well. The baby doesn't have much time left. If you and Clare want to be with him when he passes, you need to go to him now."

"How can I tell her? What can I say? He's going to die! He's not going to make it," Rodger cried.

"You can tell her, I know you can. It's not easy but you have to be strong right now for both of you. Can you do it?" Tony asked.

"You're right, somehow I will be strong." With tears in his eyes, Rodger went to Clare's bedside.

At this time, and this moment, their love became the only shield they had from the agony of losing their child. We stayed in the waiting area while the children said goodbye to Steven. He passed quietly in his mother's loving arms.

⁓   ⁓   ⁓

The following year turned into an emotional nightmare for Clare and Rodger. Her bitterness toward God, her guilt in feeling envy toward every baby and mother she came upon, Rodger's mood swings in trying to comfort each episode of his wife's grief, the two of them were on a desperate merry-go-round and couldn't get off.

Helpless, we watched our children suffer.

"It doesn't seem fair when a baby so young and innocent doesn't make it. I don't think there is anything more we can do except love them and be there for them," said Tony.

"No, it's not justifiable. Sometimes Clare used to sing 'Jesus Loves Me' for hours after Sunday school. She always had a strong faith. Where did it go? She needs it more than ever now."

"Give her time. I'm sure it will come back on its own. God is a spirit of love. She's going to feel the love again somehow."

The children met a young couple who had also lost their newborn. They strengthened each other and shared each other's pain. Slowly, mixed emotions settled down and they found peace with the world around them.

Their young love became the backbone of their survival. During the next ten years, they parented two healthy boys and one girl. Perhaps appreciating their family more than most, they were exceptional parents.

Rodger released his emotions by transferring them into his artwork. He and Tony both shared this trait. Understanding their previous losses, Rodger painted a beautiful abstract painting of a man, his wife, and their children. It hung in their living room and sent a silent message about family unity.

CHAPTER 30

My Hero

Being pulled through the woods on an emergency stretcher made from a toboggan provided for a very bumpy ride. I didn't care. My family, and Jim's dog Sport, had rescued me from an unpredictable accident.

Previously, I had seen a large patch of wild purple irises in the woods a mile from home. I had stored the idea of transplanting them into our yard. Today was a quiet day, when the weather conditions seemed perfect for gardening. I had extra time and decided to move the flowers.

Slipping into my boots, I gathered a bucket and hand spade before I went into the woods. Halfway to the flowers, the ground rapidly grabbed me into the cold wet earth. My body, from waist down, was crushed unbearably tight, as though the earth wanted to squeeze me to death. I had fallen into a black hole.

My feet dangled in a vastness of nothing. I grabbed at the grass around me to try and get traction. Maybe I could pull myself out. Useless! The grass broke apart in my hands. The more I struggled, the deeper I wedged myself. Panicked, face flushed, and body shaking with shivers, I screamed, "I'll never get out of here!" Tears streamed down my cheeks. *God, please help me. Help me get out of here.*

I yelled for help a long time; my voice became raspy then silent. There was no one to hear me. Watching the sun as it slowly sank in the western sky, I knew several hours had passed. Soon it would be dark. The muscles in my body tightened as I realized I could be any-one's or anything's prey.

I became weak and tired and watched a busy chipmunk gather food as he ran around a tree. For moments, the distraction helped me forget my crazy nightmare. My legs dangled down into space and had become numb.

Beth should be home. I hope she's looking for me. Feeling defeated, I asked God to help me before dark. Animals of the night will roam and I can't fight back.

A dog barked close by. The sound got louder. Once in my sight, I could see Jim and Vera's pooch, Sport. "Here, Sport! Come here, boy! Here, boy!" His tail wagged while he found his way to me. I petted his warm coat and talked to him.

"You're the only hope I have. Go home, tell everyone I'm here. You can do it, Sport. I know you can. Go, boy! Tell whoever you see that I'm in trouble." He licked my face and bounded off. *Could he do it? Was God going to answer my prayers through him?*

Beth had come home from school and when she finished her homework, she walked over to Vera's house to look for me.

"Hi, honey. What brings you here so late?"

"I can't find my mom. Is she here?"

"I haven't seen her all day. I'll call the station. Maybe she's with your dad. Hi, Tony. Beth is over here at our place looking for Babe. Is she there?"

"No, I talked to her early today. She planned on being home all day. Tell Beth I'll pick her up in about ten minutes." Tony sensed things weren't right. My purse sat on the table and my shoes laid on the doormat.

He and Beth started to search for me. Vera, Jim, and the boys soon joined them. Lady and Sport trailed alongside and barked non-stop. The dogs ran in erratic patterns.

"What's wrong with the dogs? They're not themselves," Tony said.

"I don't know. Never saw Sport run in circles repeatedly like this before. What is it, boy?" Jim asked.

"He's been like this for the last couple of hours. Go, Sport, go. What do you want to show us?" Vera asked.

With a drawn-out howl, Sport took off toward the woods with Lady close behind. We trampled down the brush to keep up with them. Checking often to make sure we were behind, Sport used deliberate direction to lead us closer to the disaster.

I heard the dogs bark. Maybe people are nearby! "Help! Help! I'm over here! Help!" I screamed with all my might. In minutes, the pets led the rescuers close enough to hear me. I could see Tony and the children. They ran to my side.

"Oh my god, Babe. How did you fall into the ground?" Tony asked. He put his arms around me and tried to pull me out.

"I don't know. I just fell in. Be careful, my legs are numb." Tony and Jim lifted me out slowly while Vera and the children stood, ready to help. Gently, I emerged to solid ground. My numb limbs crumbled.

"I can't feel anything from the waist down," I cried while Sport and Lady barked their victory in the background.

"Just stay where you are. I'll rub your legs and see if it helps bring the blood back. You've cut off your circulation. Just sit here on the ground until you get feeling comes back," Vera said as she continued to rub.

My limbs felt strange. First, they tingled and then ached as though they were caught in a vice. I took deep breaths to hold back tears.

"You fell into an old well someone left open. You could have been hurt worse than you are. If you would've fallen all the way down, we might not have found you," Tony said.

"Dad, I'll go get the toboggan. We can use it to pull Mom out of the woods," Robert suggested.

"Good idea. We can't drive the car in here. Tie a heavy rope on the front so we can pull it. Bring a pillow and blanket too. Your mother should not try and walk back with her legs the way they are. Do you think you can handle the toboggan, Babe?" Tony asked.

I agreed to give it a try. My journey home is one I'll always remember. The bumpy ground caused me to fall off my chariot multiple times, but it did carry me back safely. Sport became my hero. If it wasn't for that spunky pet, I may not have been found in time to avoid serious physical injury. There's always an extra treat for him and a prayer of thanks for sending this unlikely hero to rescue me.

CHAPTER 31

Unanimous Vote

Applause and cheers could be heard from the opposite end of town. The greatest little town show ever performed just finished their finale. Clumsy curtsies were made by the cast. The joyful throng prevailed until the sky darkened enough for a fireworks display.

Granite's traditional Fourth of July celebration is looked forward to by hundreds of tourist and residents alike. A parade in the morning, vendor crafts and children's games in the afternoon, and a hilarious pageant at the end of the day, closing with a fireworks show in the evening. Tents and booths offered favorite picnic food and treats. There was no better recipe for a family fun day.

"The boys aren't little anymore. They're old enough to take part in the Stump Dump Pageant. Let's ask them to volunteer with us this year. Beth's old enough to help with costumes and stage props. All of the kids could be helpful," I suggested.

"Sounds like a good idea. I can see the boys in skirts. I'll have to try not to laugh," Tony said.

"Maybe they would want us to laugh. Isn't that the whole idea?"

"Yeah maybe. What would you think if I want to be Nancy Sinatra this year? You know, 'Those Boots Were Made for Walkin'?'"

"We could do it. We'll make you gorgeous," I answered.

The Stump Dump Pageant is a unique event. Men from town come together to individually imitate a famous woman singer. Today it's called lip-synching. The production is well-attended. Ticket sales collect a hefty amount of charitable dollars for the children's cancer camps in our area. These muscular men are not graceful, and they are funny to watch as they try to be feminine for the show.

We asked the boys and Beth if they would like to volunteer with us for this year's production. Much to my surprise, they jumped at the idea.

"I want to be Judy Garland and sing 'Somewhere Over the Rainbow,'" Bob announced.

"I'll do Shirley Temple doing 'On the Good Ship Lollipop,'" Anthony said.

"I want to be a stagehand and help you, Mom," Beth chimed in. With all this enthusiasm, the pageant was bound to be a success.

Volunteers were surprised when town officials informed them the community center gym, where we held our past performances, had been outgrown. We were expected to exceed the fire code with the number of people allowed inside the building at one time. The participants decided to hold the show outside in Granite's park.

Plans to build a stage were discussed. Tony, Jim, and a half-dozen men from town offered to build one. Construction had begun as soon as the winter snow melted. Finished in June, the generous-sized wooden stage had a solid cement foundation and an adequate protective canopy. Large portable folding partitions cuddled the platform on each side to give entertainers an unseen place to wait for their entrance. Built on high ground with surrounding grass, the stratum beckoned the audience yet to come.

Beth and I helped the men in our family to gather the things they needed for costumes: wigs, dresses, a cowgirl outfit, red-painted slippers, white boots, and lollipops. With the use of two blue-and-white check tablecloths, Bob's Dorothy dress looked authentic. The cowgirl costume for Tony required a white vest and shorts to match his white boots. Anthony's frock, with pink ruffles, complemented the Shirley Temple look.

The day of the pageant, Beth and I did all we could to help our men get ready. Wigs and makeup were applied last. Our nonstop laughing couldn't be helped. All three guys looked outlandish.

Waiting in the wings behind the stage presented a problem the planning committee hadn't foreseen. Mosquitoes were there in abundance. Beth had some bug repellent and sprayed the area. Smacking and scratching dislocated some of the padding used to form the men's feminine shapes, and with no time to redress, their stage entrances were greeted with hysterics.

Tony's voice cracked while he sang "These Boots Were Made for Walkin'." He couldn't help laughing as he pushed up his front anatomy. His wig fell lopsided when he stomped in his boots.

Bobby did well to entertain the audience when the bale of hay he tried to sit on fell over. Getting up, he started to sing "Somewhere Over the Rainbow" and he found he lost a red slipper. His dress had torn on one side and his petticoat dragged on the floor. Beth and I laughed so much our cheeks hurt.

When Anthony made his entrance, all seemed well until he started to tap dance while eating his enormous lollipop. It fell and he tried to pick it up, but bending over caused his wig to fall off and part of his padding to shift. This bald Shirley Temple continued to lick her sucker and dance.

After the fireworks, we went home laughing, hungry, and tired. Removing their stage outfits helped the boys to unwind and bologna sandwiches and cold milk stopped the hunger growls.

"It's still hot and humid. Let's go down to the pier and dangle our feet in the water. We need to cool down before bed," Tony said. One by one, we walked to the dock and sat alongside one another.

"You all were terrific tonight. I don't remember when I had as much fun as I did today. So glad you all came this year," I said.

"How about if we do it again next year?" Anthony said.

"I'll second it," Bob answered.

"Me too," Beth echoed.

"Mom and I say yes. The vote's unanimous," Tony clarified.

Ready for a good night's sleep, we left one by one to go back to the house. Thoughts of next year's Fourth of July's fabrication invaded our dreams.

CHAPTER 32

For Our Children's Sake

Down on my red scruffy knees, I removed the old wax from each 12×12 floor tile embedded in my kitchen floor. How dingy they looked without their shine.

The radio, neatly mounted in our paneled wall, played light classic tunes, mostly Peter Paul and Mary. In order to change my nasty job into a somewhat tolerable experience, I sang like an imaginable star. I had no audience, but I bellowed the words to "Puff the Magic Dragon" over and over again.

A broadcast unexpectedly caught my attention. A man's serious monotone voice said, "We interrupt this program for a news bulletin. The president has been shot!"

What did I hear? Again, the announcer said, "The president has been shot! I repeat, the president has been shot!" In disbelief, I stopped work and focused on the radio. This couldn't happen here in the United States. It happens in other countries, not ours. I got off the floor and moved closer to the radio to listen.

The news continued. "Our reporter, who is at the scene, reports the president is being rushed to Parkland Hospital in Dallas, Texas. Mrs. Kennedy is at his side. We will inform you as the news reaches our newsroom. Stay tuned for updates. I repeat, the president has been shot!"

Had our handsome red-headed president, John F. Kennedy, really been shot? How serious is his injury? Who did this?

Tony called to find out if I knew about the shooting. "I'm listening to the reports right now. Are you?" I asked.

"Yes, I am. It must be true because everyone who comes in for gas has their radio turned up loud. It's hard to believe. I'll see you later, if the world doesn't blow up first."

There were breaks between broadcasts. Information came in slow. The radio spokesperson gave details over and over to reassure listeners updates would continue. Eventually the news broke.

"The president and Mrs. Kennedy, along with Governor John Connally and his wife, Nellie, were traveling in an open convertible car in a motorcade parade through the streets of Dallas. While they waved to roadside supporters, shots were fired, hitting the president and governor. President Kennedy slumped over close to the side of his wife, Jacqueline. Their car is speeding to get to a trauma center. Vice President Johnson trails three cars behind. As more news breaks, we will report."

Our backdoor slammed open, almost hitting the wall. "Gosh, Tony, take it easy. You almost knocked the door off its hinges."

"Sorry! Turn on the television!"

"Okay. What's the rush?"

"It's all on TV. Turn off the radio. We can watch it as it happens," Tony said as he reached to turn the set on. We stood side by side close to the screen, our eyes fixed on the journalist that was now at the scene. Crowds surrounded the medical facility, waiting for word on the condition of the president. The camera roamed through bystanders, catching them looking toward the doors with tears in their eyes.

"I still can't believe this! Only barbaric people settle things with guns. We're not like this, are we?" I asked.

"We only know what goes on in our own little world. Don't kid yourself. There is violence everywhere."

"This scares me. I have always felt safe here. Am I a Pollyanna or something?"

"No, but maybe a little naive. There's hate in this world around us."

Feeling venerable, I moved up close to Tony and wrapped my arms around his waist. He put his arm around me, and I felt safe again.

We sat on the couch and watched history unravel in front of an audience of millions. Men in white doctor's coats appeared at the door of the emergency entrance of the trauma center. They signaled to reporters and well-wishers to be silent. We watched intensely.

"The president was pronounced dead in Trauma Room One at 12:30 p.m. from a gunshot wound to the head. Mrs. Kennedy is with him. Governor Connally is being treated in Trauma Room Two. He is in critical condition," reported the journalist.

The bystanders began to disperse. The broadcast switched over to the news channel we always watched.

"Isn't this awful?" I said.

"Leave the set on in case any more comes on. With the president dead, the vice president should be taking office, and I don't want to miss anything. Tony stayed by the TV while I went about my household tasks.

"I left a note at the station for the boys to come home when they come in after school. They should be here to follow the broadcasts. Mike said he would drive them," Tony said.

"Good. We'll have an early dinner and eat in the front room." When Robert and Anthony arrived, they joined us.

Bobby said, "Don't worry about closing early, Dad. There isn't any business anyway. Everybody is home glued to their TVs."

"Good. I figured so. I want you all to witness this."

When dinnertime came, we carried our plates of food into the front room, sat close to the coffee table, and ate while we watched. Vice President Lyndon Johnson automatically became the thirty-sixth president of the United States when President Kennedy died. Reporters filled the airways with an account of the changeover.

The president's plane, known as Air Force One, transported the deceased president's body, from Dallas to Washington D.C. Mrs. Kennedy accompanied her late husband on his final journey. Vice President Lyndon Johnson traveled with them. At 2:38 p.m. on the same day, Johnson's swearing-in ceremony took place onboard the flight.

"Do you boys know anything about our new president?" Tony asked.

"Not really," Bob said.

"How about you, Anthony?"

"I've heard of him. I knew about Kennedy."

"Beth, do you understand what happened to President Kennedy?"

"He got shot and died," Beth said.

"Right. It's not every day this happens to our president. In all of our US history, there have been four presidents assassinated, counting Kennedy," Tony said.

"Who killed him?" asked Anthony.

"We're waiting to hear. There is always someone trying to assassinate the president. There are a lot of sick-minded people doing bad things. We don't realize this because we live here, far away from big cities. When towns are large, they have a lot of people and it is more likely someone is mentally ill. Someone who is mentally ill is not able to tell right from wrong," Tony answered.

"I remember an odd conversation I had with a man at our last church dinner. His wife and I talked about how much we approved of President Kennedy. Interrupting, her husband said that President Kennedy is the only president this country ever had who is Catholic. He said he'll never make it."

"What do you mean?" I asked.

"He'll never make it."

"What does religion have to do with the presidency?"

"Mark my words. He's Catholic. I had shrugged it off as a remark made by someone who doesn't know what they're talking about. Now I am beginning to wonder."

"Do any of you think guys think there is a religious supremacy movement in this country?" I asked. The children shrugged their shoulders as if to say, "We don't know."

We left our television console turned on all of the time except when we slept. Repeated reports played over and over until a piece of new information interrupted the screen. Seventy hours after the murder, an ex-marine named Lee Harvey Oswald became the number one suspect of the murders. He had a quiet demure, and it seemed hard to think of him as a killer. Arrested on two counts of murder, he denied any wrongdoing.

Three shots were reported to have been fired. One is believed to have killed Officer Tippit of the Dallas Police Force, the second to have shot the president, and the third had hit Governor Connally. News personnel said Lee Harvey Oswald acted on his own although latter reports stated a possible conspiracy.

A quick arrest temporarily placed Oswald in a county jail. The plan was to transfer him to a city jail within two days. With TV cameras rolling, he attempted to make the exit. A Dallas nightclub owner named Jack Ruby ambushed Oswald and shot him to death in front of millions of Americans watching their televisions.

"Come here. Oswald's shot, he's dead," yelled Tony. The children and I ran into the front room.

"What happened?" I asked. Tony told us as we watched the screen. I covered my mouth to keep from yelling. "This can't be true."

"The world's gone crazy," Tony said. With eyes as big as raccoons, our children watched the murder play out on the world's stage, over and over.

The following three days, every channel on our RCA broadcast the wake and burial of the slain president. America wept. Our country's peaceful innocence became tarnished. I feared guns would rule here again as they did some 150 years ago. Our country's involvement in the Vietnam War became unfavorable with the American people. Citizens became divided about its purpose. Racial intolerances were at a peak and civil unrest became a constant voice.

These times led us into a world of intolerance for our fellow man instead of loving and caring for them. Will our nation, under God, return to its once respectful and peaceful existence? For our children's sake, it has to. But when?

CHAPTER 33

We'll Make It Work

Bob and Anthony being robbed made me mad. It happened at a beautiful lake in Canada, where one is supposed to find peace. I wanted to punch the thieves silly. The thieves, being adults, knew what they were doing. How could they do this to a couple of kids? What a nasty disillusionment for our boys.

When Robert and Anthony graduated from high school, one year apart, Tony and I preached about college.

"You need to go. You might regret it later if you don't. You'll need to make money to care for your families and your body does wear out as you get older. This day will come, and you need to be realistic about your future. A job using your head, instead of your back, will make a difference. Good jobs require college," Tony preached.

Both boys decided to stay home and continue their jobs at our service station. Bobby made clear his preference. "I like it here. I'm tired of school, and my girlfriend Margie lives in town. Don't be upset if I don't want to go to college. School bores me. I don't want to bother with it."

Anthony echoed his response with one additional thought. "Someday, I want to buy Dad's station and keep it in the family. I love mechanics."

Even though it would be financially difficult for us to send them to college at the same time, we would have found a way and were disappointed in their choices.

141

"They like to fish. I'm going to suggest a vacation. Out on a lake with a rod in hand is a good time to think about things. Who knows? They might change their minds. A break has been well earned anyway," Tony said.

Arrangements were made for their absence from work. We liked the plans they made to go north. In June, the ice melts off the Canadian lakes. The game fish are hungry and will bite nonstop. Someone can reach their fish limit in a couple of hours.

So when the Canadian fishing season opened, Robert and Anthony packed their gear. Both had excellent casting rods and complete tackle boxes. Tony suggested they take our forty-horsepower boat motor.

You could see the excitement in their smiles when they drove away in Bobby's 1965 Ford Fairlane. With no one else to consider but themselves, they blasted their favorite music all the way to the border. Once across, they found a resort on a chain of seven lakes. The owner welcomed them and rented the brothers a two-bedroom cottage and a boat. They parked alongside the quarters while they unloaded luggage and three boxes of groceries.

"I'm hungry. Do you want some of these cheese crackers?" Anthony asked.

"Yeah, give me some. Let's go out early tomorrow and scout out the lakes. It's legal to troll in Canada. We can set the motor on slow and drag our lines." Going to bed early, they were prepared to get up at dawn.

In the morning, anticipation went with them as they launched their boat. With the motor mounted securely, they pushed off onto the lake, ready for action. Scouting the area became an adventure of its own.

While they roamed the waters, thick cloud cover darkened the sky, and it began to rain.

"Did we bring ponchos?" Anthony asked.

"We did."

The motor suddenly stopped. It jolted them as though they were on rides in an amusement park. With surprised looks on their faces, Robert and Anthony checked for the cause.

"It's broke. Look at the pin. Completely stripped. Now what?" Bob said.

"I don't even know where we're at. Do you?" asked Anthony.

"We got off the main track somewhere along the way. The weather is getting nasty. Look at those waves. They're getting bigger by the minute. Did we bring a compass?" asked Bobby.

"I've got one in my tackle box."

"Good."

"What the ———. It's not here!" exclaimed Anthony.

"Without direction, we'll never find our way back. I only see shoreline," Bob said. "We can row over to it."

"The water is rough. I'm not sure we can make it." They struggled with the oars trying to gain control of the boat.

"I think I see a cabin. Let's try and make it there," Bob said. The winds howled. The rain beat upon their faces and ran down their necklines, soaking their shirts. The heavy downpour limited their view to twenty feet. Every muscle in their arms screamed while they used all of their strength to push against the oars.

"We're going in circles. What should we do? "Anthony said.

"Maybe we better wait for the storm to pass."

"My hands are raw from the darn oars."

"Mine too. Let's just sit quiet until the rain lets up again and we can see the cottage." Lightning and thunder surrounded them. One strike after another rumbled and shook their boat to the core.

"Are we in hell?" Anthony said.

"I don't know, but if we make it to shore, it will be some kind of miracle."

For an hour, the storm raged on. Both were ready to panic and lost confidence as sailors. "We better bail some of the water out of the boat. It's deep on the floor. This is the pits," Bob said.

"Bail with what?"

"Empty out the milk bottle. I'll use the bait bucket."

"Don't dump the minnows!"

"I have to. We're in trouble. We can always get more." The water receded as fast as they scooped.

"I can see the cabin. Look!" Anthony said.

"To the left. What have we got to lose? Let's go for it." Taking turns with the oars and with bursts of energy, they began to make headway.

"How are we going to get the boat up on shore with all those rocks?"

"I don't know until we get there," Bob said. As they approached, the sailors could see the water covered a rocky terrain. The closer they came, the smaller the rocks appeared. While moving with the waves to shore, the rock sizes diminished to gravel.

"I didn't think we had a chance of landing without damage."

"Me either. Better pull the boat up away from the shoreline." They found trees on the sandy beach to tie their boat.

"I hope somebody is home in the cottage," Anthony said.

"If not, we're going in anyway. It's a matter of life and death for us to find shelter. This storm is wicked, and it's not over yet. The fact we didn't get hit by a lightning bolt is a surprise to me."

"Yeah, but it's against the law to break in."

"I don't care. I'll leave a note with my phone number and pay for any damage we do or anything we use." Bob walked over to a nearby woodpile where he found a hand-sized rock. Using the rock as a tool, he pounded open the flimsy metal lock on the front door. It burst and shattered across the porch.

"I hope you know what you're doing," Anthony criticized.

Exhausted and soaked, with hands swollen and blistered, the scavengers entered the oasis. There were two bedrooms with full-sized beds. Both boys adopted a place to rest and fell asleep as soon as they closed their eyes. All fears were temporarily extinguished, like a fire put out with a hose.

Early the next day, after fifteen hours of sleep, song birds woke them up from their slumber.

"Wonder if there is any food around here?" Bob said while he searched the kitchen. Anthony found a fully stocked pantry. They both indulged until satisfied.

"From what I remember Dad teaching us, green moss on a tree trunk always faces north. The sun comes up in the east and works its way west for the sunset. When the sun is directly overhead, it's noon."

"I think you're right. I remember too," Anthony said.

"Let's clean up here, leave a note, and try to fix the front door so it stays shut. The sooner we get started, the better. There are some rubber gloves on the dish drainer. Let's cover our hands with Vaseline from our tackle boxes and put the mitts on to protect them. We still have to row for miles today," said Bob.

While still early morn, they studied the tree moss and the position of the sun to decide the direction to travel. The lads remembered their rented cottage faced the north. Straight south would be the course back.

Shoreline trees were checked for moss every two hours. The intervals were found to be a good time to switch rowers. Their hands still hurt even though they were protected, but both of the boys knew they must go on. To find their way back meant their survival.

Wildlife seemed abundant as they pushed through the waters. Bears, coons, deer, moose, eagles, and owls covered the shoreline. Upon dusk, signs of civilization appeared. Buildings and boat docks polka-dotted the terrain. Against odds, they had made it back before dark.

Tired, aching, and in pain, they entered their cabin, ready to collapse. After eating, with clothes still on their backs, they fell into the nearest beds and drifted into a deep sleep.

In the morning, Bob laid quietly and listened to music while he fought to open his eyes. Confused, he wondered where the music came from. Realizing it came from his car radio, he jumped to his feet. Startled by a tree trunk lying across the kitchen ceiling, he yelled, "What happened? Anthony, where are you? Where are you?"

His brother stumbled into the kitchen, saying, "Here, right here." It didn't take them long to realize severe thunderstorms had taken place while they slept. They didn't hear the storms because of their exhaustion.

A tree jutted out the side of the cottage, draping itself over the top of their car. Both the car roof and the windshield were flattened like an ironed shirt. The music from the car radio continued to blare.

Bob dug his way into the tree rubbish that was scattered across the car to turn the radio off.

"I'm surprised the radio didn't break. What a mess!" said Bob.

The resort owner did all he could to help the boys and let them use his phone to call home. Tony suggested the boys take the car to the junkyard, but with no car title, the cost would be outlandishly high in Canada.

"See if it runs. If you can drive it back to the USA, you won't need the title to junk it, and you'll have cash for plane tickets home," Tony said.

With their mechanical expertise, the brothers fixed the car enough to run, but the smashed windshield became a problem. It was against the law to drive with a shattered windshield in Canada.

"You can see out over the broken windows. There are only fragments of glass left. We'll have to take our chances we don't get stopped. We've got to get home," Anthony said.

The resort manager offered his motorcycle goggles for their safety. "Let's take the remains of broken glass out of the windshield. With it gone we should be okay," Bob said.

While they worked on the car, a couple from the USA staying at the resort introduced themselves. They lived in a small town not far from where we lived. A welcome coincidence. They offered to bring the motor and gear back home for the boys. This solved their problem of how to transport things home. The car's broken body left no room to securely pack. After their "thank you" and exchange of addresses and phone numbers, our young men waved goodbye and drove their noisy crumbling car out of the resort and headed home to the USA.

There was no problem at the border. After facts were checked; the inspectors let them through. Finding a populated area, they found a junkyard. Their dad had figured right: the car sold for enough money for plane tickets home, with some money left over. The junkyard owners let the boys use their phone to make flight arrangements and call home. The leftover money paid for lunch and a cab ride to the airport.

When Tony and I picked the boys up from the airport, I hardly recognized them. Both had cruddy wrinkled clothes on and stubby beards. Could these be the smiling young men we watched drive out of our driveway?

I hugged them. It felt as good as whipped cream on strawberry shortcake. When we left the airport, I watched our two young men walk away with their father. It warmed my heart as I realized the boys and Tony all had the same gait. Their strut seemed masculine the way they swayed their arms. I adored them in the way a mother feels when her newborn is placed in her arms for the first time.

Two days later, they went together to pick up their gear and motor. The address and phone number given to them by the nice couple in Canada were fake. My young explorers had been robbed in a disguise of compassion. We were all angry. We ranted and raved while we tried every way we knew of to find the thieves. They had covered their tracks well. The stolen goods were never to be recovered.

Eventually a conversation about college took place.

"I still don't want to go. There are no classes anywhere to teach what we learned on our trip. This town and the station are my world and I want to keep it this way," said Bob.

"I still want to buy your station, Dad. Can we work it out in some way?" asked Anthony.

In acceptance of their decisions, Tony said, "Yep, we'll make it work."

CHAPTER 34

Beth's Place

Suicide? At our station? Unthinkable!

At 2:00 a.m. the phone rang. Tony and I bumped into each other to reach the unexpected sound. We knocked the phone on the floor and bumped heads.

Still dazed, Tony said, "Hello?"

"Tony Weston?" the caller asked.

"Yes."

"I'm Charlie from the county police. We're at your station. A man jumped through your station's window and killed himself. You need to come and board up your windows," he said.

"Is this really you, Charlie? What made him do such a terrible thing?"

"We don't know yet. We need you here as soon as possible."

"Give me five minutes to get dressed and I'll leave," Tony answered. After Tony explained the call and dressed in record time, he left before I could process all he had told me. I didn't know any further details until Anthony and Bob took me along with them at 8:00 a.m. for their regular day shift.

When we arrived, the intruder's body had been taken away by the coroner and the police were gone. At this time, no one knew why this man had jumped through our window. We all shook our heads in disbelief and went about our daily station routines. What really happened?

Two days later, a young blonde woman with an infant in her arms, perhaps in her twenties, walked into our station office.

"I'd like to speak to the owner please," she said. Tony and I were both behind the desk at the time.

Tony answered, "I'm the owner. Can I help you?"

"My name is Judy Marshall. I am the wife of the man who jumped through your window. I would like to pay you for the damage he caused. I don't have much, but I could make small payments every month to cover the cost.

"He finally made it. He tried to kill himself once before and jumped off a rooftop. This time, we were camped at the campground when he disappeared. He had a few beers but did not seem depressed. I didn't know where he had gone. I heard about the jump from some campers and thought it might be him. I went to the police station. This is how I found out. I want to be responsible for his damage."

"We're so sorry. You don't owe me anything. My insurance will pay for a new window. Where are you from?" Tony asked.

"Ohio."

"Are you and your baby okay? Would you like to use our phone to call family or a friend?" I asked.

"The police were very kind and they helped me contact family. My mom and dad are coming."

"I'm glad. Have a safe trip home."

The young woman walked to her car and left. We never heard another word about the incident. Our insurance did replace the window. After a few weeks, the memory of this sad event stored itself in the back of our minds.

Anthony wanted to buy our station. He had mentioned this several times. Tony and I decided it would benefit all of us if we made that change.

"You've pushed yourself to work and you need to consider retirement. It would be nice if we had more time together before we get too old to enjoy it. Things would change for the better. You won't have to set the alarm for 5:00 a.m. You could spend more time in your workshop," I bartered.

"You're right. It's about time. The boys are old enough to carry the load. I would like to go in once in a while. I can't leave altogether. I'll gradually cut the ties. We should talk with a representative from the bank and find out what our options are. I'm sure we can work things out," Tony said.

The business end of our plan went well. Everyone involved seemed pleased with the outcome. Anthony became the new owner.

"Thanks, Dad. We'll keep it going. Bob is well organized, and he'll make sure the bank, books, and supplies are taken care of. I don't know how to deal with the oil company reps. I'll have questions and will need your advice on that."

"I know you will. If you need me and I'm not around the shop, you can always call. You're the best mechanic I've ever known, and Bob knows how we managed things. You two will do just fine," Tony said.

With the deal closed, Tony and I were ready for retirement.

After six months, we found ourselves frustrated trying to adjust to each other's routines. It took me a while to learn to react to Tony's on-the-spur-of-the-moment routine. Tony would decide to go somewhere and announce his plans on his way to the car. Used to my own routine, I found it hard to stop on a moment's notice.

Tony wrestled with the idea that I would be with him every time he went somewhere. After the first year, we figured out the necessity of togetherness and, at the same time, the importance of our own identities.

We were older than Vera and Jim, but the age difference didn't hinder our friendship. A good laugh came from all when we gloated about the *good retirement life*.

"Some people, like me, don't have to get up early every morning to go to work. We just sleep in and take time to cook delicious big breakfasts every day," teased Tony.

"We can go anywhere anytime we see fit," I bragged.

Jim and Vera joked along with us.

One evening, Tony called me to come sit with him. "Come here, Babe, I want to talk to you about an idea I have."

"You sound so serious. What's on your mind?"

"I'd like to build a cottage close to the lake. A beach-type house. Beth graduates from high school soon and talks about her own place. She could live in the cottage if she wants to. If not, we could use it for family or rent it out. I plan on a three-bedroom ranch. What do you think?"

"Do you really want to take on a project this big? And do we have the money to do it?" I asked.

"I think we can afford it. I'm going to take my time and spread the work over a two-year period. I've got to find a way to keep busy. I'm tired of no routine."

"I could work on it too. The kids are gone from home a lot. The boys plan to move into their own place this year," I said.

Tony felt challenged and grinned from ear to ear. He had a newfound skip in his walk. Happy and ready to build, he applied for permits. Carefully, he put his plans in script and ordered materials from Jim's store. Both Jim and Vera volunteered to help. Our place once again became busy with accomplishment.

After the foundation dried on the cottage, his dream house began to take shape. Tony had his workshop in an additional space added onto the back of our garage, so tools were always at his fingertips. The sound of power tools and hammer knocks echoed. Jim and Vera spent several hours a week on our project. The four of us put the new dwelling under roof before winter.

"Are you going to give the cottage a name?" Vera asked.

"How about Beth's Place?" Tony suggested.

We nodded our heads in approval, and the vote became unanimous.

"That name is perfect. Beth's Place it is," I confirmed.

CHAPTER 35

Our Rock

Seeing Tony with torn flesh that was saturated with blood made me nauseated. How could he let something like this happen? He didn't do it on purpose, so why did I feel like I want to run away? I can't handle something like this. It's horrible! I should have never left him alone.

Vera and Jim were always over to help us work on Beth's Place. You could see our breath while we scurried around, trying to keep warm. With no heat, we used a space heater. It barely took away the chill. I didn't tolerate the cold very well, so working on household tasks that day were a good excuse for me to procrastinate on my share of work. Jim and Vera were helping despite the frigid temps. Truer friends could never be had.

The next day, Tony and I planned to work alone. For a short time, I stayed back to do housework. I vacuumed. When finished with the housework, it seemed odd not to hear sounds of power tools or music. Tony always blasted his radio when he worked alone. This is strange! I decided to check out the silence.

I listened close to the garage and my ears picked up a weak call for help. Startled, I flung open the garage service door.

"Thank God you heard me. Help me. I thought you would never stop vacuuming," Tony whimpered.

"Your hand. What happened to your right hand?"

"I cut off the end of my fingers and thumb. Get some towels. Hurry up, I'm bleeding bad."

I ran in the house and grabbed an armful of bath towels. Quickly, I wrapped some of them around his injured hand. It didn't take long for the blood to soak through.

"Get me to the hospital," Tony barely said. He looked faint.

We arrived at the hospital within twenty minutes. The towels were blood-soaked. Emergency room staff surrounded Tony while I looked on in shock. *Did this really happen? It can't be. He's worked around machinery and tools for years. What happened?*

While the doctors treated Tony, I waited in the hospital hall. When the medical team finished, they allowed me to return close to Tony's gurney.

Pain relieved, Tony said, "When I cut a beam on the band saw, I forgot the safety switch. My thumb and first three fingers on my right hand got caught." I smiled and told him everything will be all right. But as I acted out this reassurance, I became nauseous. The sight of his bloody stumped fingers made me feel sick. *I've got to deal with this! He can't see me rejecting the sight of his hand!*

It seemed hours before the doctor bandaged Tony's injury. The physician said, "I would like to keep him overnight to make sure he's stable."

"This sounds like a good idea. I'll come back early tomorrow to bring him home," I answered. When hospital visiting hours were over, I left Tony with words of encouragement and comfort even though I wanted to scream.

The emotional stress of the day had left me exhausted. When I returned home, I had a long private cry and then let Vera, Jim, and our children know what happened. Their support provided reassurance that all would be well.

The cleanup of the shop where the accident took place plagued my mind. I knew it had to be done and forced myself to do it. Tony must not return to the raw sight of his accident. Cleaning the dried blood from the saw and floor wasn't as bad as I thought it would be. When I picked up his torn-flesh fingertips, his nails were still in place. I sobbed and almost collapsed. *How horrible! How could this happen to my tower of strength?*

Half dazed, I walked in circles, not knowing how to dispose them. I cried and went outside, dug a small hole, and buried them. When finished, I closed the door to the garage and hoped to shut out the memory of this horrid day.

In the morning, I went back to the hospital. A nurse sat down with us and explained how I should care for Tony's hand. The sight of his ragged fleshy wounds made me sick to my stomach again. *Would this happen every time I dressed his wounds?* I did my best to hide it from him.

Positive thinking and encouragement were necessities for a good outcome for Tony. The nurse set up several appointments for Tony to meet with a hand therapist. I was thankful that Tony had taught me to drive. It made me happy to be able to take him to doctor and clinic visits. The only important thing to me was Tony's recovery.

"Babe, you've been wonderful. I'm almost useless, and you take such good care of me. Thank you, sweetheart! I hate to see you overworked."

"I'm okay. I know you would do the same for me, wouldn't you? You're my world, Tony. There is no one or anything more important to me than you."

"We have to be realistic. I'm not going to be able to do all of the things I used to be able to do."

"So what? As long as you're here with me, I'll be fine. I can't get along without you. Besides, you'll come out of this better than you think," I said.

Eventually Tony's wounds healed. New flesh grew across his fingertips. He made jokes about his stubby stumps. Holding a stump finger to his nose gave the appearance of a half finger being up his nose. He laughed like crazy every time he did it.

"I'm going to try and work on Beth's Place. Don't know if I can, but I'm going to try," Tony said.

"You're stubborn, and you'll figure it out if you have to stand on your head." I laughed.

"I'm not so sure this time. Who can do anything with one hand?"

"You can. I know you'll find new ways. I've seen your creative juices flow when you figure out how to paint on canvas with stubby fingers. Your new picture of Beth's Place is a keepsake."

"You're my rock," Tony said.

"And you are mine."

CHAPTER 36

Just You and Me

Sweating profusely woke me. *Why? I need my sleep to get over this teary-eyed state I walk in every day. This stinkin' thinkin' has got to stop! Now I'm shaking with cold. What's going on?*

The first time I noticed my moody behavior, I had been talking to Bobby and Anthony about their plans to rent or buy a home. They were ready to take on the world on their own, but there's not much to choose from in our area. Anthony had talked to a customer at the station who mentioned he was looking for a buyer for his small house in town because the company he worked for required relocation in another state. "I'm ready to sell it far below market price. I have a deadline to meet in New York. I want it gone before then. You wouldn't happen to know anyone looking to buy a house, would you?" he asked.

"I might. My brother and I have been looking for a place of our own. Where is it located? What size is it? Does it have two bathrooms? How many bedrooms?"

Arrangements were made for a buyers' walk-through.

The home was located close to the station and our house, and this made a possible purchase desirable. Tony, me, and the boys went together to examine the possibilities. To our surprise, it fits their needs and budget. The deal on the new man cave closed six weeks later. Before taking possession, they managed to paint and furnish their new habitat.

Clare and Rodger came in to help them move. Jim, Vera, Tony, and I helped as well. By late afternoon on move day, we were done. To conclude the day, we celebrated their brave move by going to town together for supper. The brothers were excited to be on their own.

When we returned home, the reality of two more of my children being gone didn't sit very well. Teary-eyed, I said, "Do you realize there's only three of us in this big house? The kids are grown. Even you, Beth. Before Dad and I know it, you'll be gone."

"Don't worry about me leaving for a while, Mom. I want to become a nurse, and I plan on going to junior college for two years, so I will stay at home. And I still have my senior year in high school to finish," she answered.

"The house seems so big, and it's spooky quiet," I whimpered.

"Beth, I'm going to finish Beth's Place this year. Don't forget it will be available to you if you want to use it," Tony said as he put his arm around me. He knew I missed the boys.

I needed to learn to cook for three. I mashed too many potatoes every time I made them and always had leftover meat. It became a challenge to cook the right amounts. Tony and I were the only two at the table most of the time, as Beth was always active and rarely took time to sit down for a meal.

"I guess I could take leftovers and drop them off at the boys' house," I said.

"They buy and eat junk food. I would be surprised if they bothered with meals. Maybe you better ask them first," Tony suggested.

"I hope they don't eat like that. I thought I taught them better." I allowed myself to mope around with tears in my eyes. It wasn't a common behavior for me. After a few weeks, I realized I still had a purpose and snapped myself out of the stinkin' thinkin'. My children have grown up and don't need me much anymore.

My unpredictable behavior and swings in body temperature must be what women call the "change of life." The symphony of voices faded away and in its place was an abundance of memories. Now was the time for me to spend extra time with Tony and enjoy a home with straightened drawers and a lack of clutter.

Tony continued to try and master new skills with his untrained fingertips. He made progress when he learned to hold objects firmly with his right hand by wrapping the injured stubs around them. His hand strength returned. If he could adjust, so could I.

Vera and Jim came over regularly to help finish up Beth's Place.

"It's starting to look like a house inside. What have you planned to cover the floors with?" asked Vera.

"Floor tiles in the kitchen, and to make it easier to finish up, we'll use indoor-outdoor carpeting on the rest of the floors. It will be less stress for Tony's hand and sturdy underfoot," I said.

"Good idea. Warmer in the winter too."

Tony and Jim put up the drywall and plastered the seams. Vera and I helped sand them smooth. "I'm not going to make the kitchen cabinets like I originally planned. We'll buy them already made. Can you order some for me through the store, Jim?" Tony asked.

"Sure, I can. They're on sale in the spring."

When it came time for installation, Jim and Vera's boys and ours helped us hang them. Tony and Jim found the overhead work to be hard.

"Guess we're getting old. My shoulder has been hurting since we hung the bedroom doors," Jim complained, half laughing.

"Thought I'd never see the day I couldn't nail a cabinet up higher than my head." Tony laughed.

"You're not the only ones. I'm having a heck of a time getting up off of the floor." Vera giggled.

"Maybe it's time we think about retirement too," Jim said. After comparing aches and pains, the four of us agreed a slower routine with less physical work would suit us better.

Over the next three months, we worked on finishing the cottage. Vera and I spent hours planning the selection of furniture and window treatments. When completed, the *cozy look* said *welcome*. We were glad to be done and looked forward to our newfound slower pace.

Tony and I found aging together to be a surprisingly beautiful time in our lives. A deeper level of affection for one another emerged. Underlying peace with unselfish love and respect prevailed, and the importance of tangible possessions faded away. Self no longer existed. All we cared about was each other.

~　　~　　　~

The lake appeared very inviting. Tony said, "I'll help you clean up after supper. Then let's go out for walleye. We can go before dark."

"Our supply of fish is low, so that's a good idea. The sunset is beautiful too."

We used the canoe to glide quietly around the marshy shoreline. Cricket sounds and splashing water during a catch carried halfway across the lake. A loon sang its bedtime song; and the sunset of pink, red, and orange filled the sky while the colors slowly faded away. The peacefulness enriched our souls.

"I wonder if heaven is as beautiful as being on the lake. You know, we're both Ig darn old. It won't be long before it's our turn. Where did the time go?" Tony said.

"I don't know! You turn around; and all of a sudden, the kids are gone, and there you are, too darn old to jitterbug."

"You nut. Who should worry about a dance? I think about us dying and one of us being here without the other someday. I can't bear the thought," Tony answered.

"You have to. The kids will be here to help whoever remains. You can't deny the truth. It's the cycle of life."

"It's hard to talk about. I don't know if I can," Tony answered.

"Don't be afraid. Whoever goes first will wait for the other. Our love is forever, honey. I know it. Our souls will always be together," I said.

"I suppose, but I don't want to think about it. I've always said, life is like a book with many chapters. We're starting another now. I can't help but wonder how it will end."

"It's not for us to know until we pass. Jesus promises us life after death in a wonderful place with Him. We have to trust His word. Let's enjoy what time we have here now, like in the beginning—you, me, and nobody else."

The End

About the Author

J oanne Schehl wrote this novel to promote the beauty of a simple
life with the glory of nature. She would like to pass on the joy she
lived in doing so. A great-great-grandmother, now retired, she shares
this story written for your enjoyment.

CPSIA information can be obtained
at www.ICGtesting.com
Printed in the USA
LVHW011953310721
694026LV00010B/785